THE PIED PUNCH AND JUDY MAN
Book Three of the Runford Chronicles
by

Rex Merchant

Copyright © Rex Merchant   2000
ISBN   9781902474069

First edition 2000
Published by
Rex Merchant @ Norman Cottage
89 West Road
OAKHAM
Rutland
LE15 6LT UK

British   Library   Cataloguing-in-Publication Data. A catalogue record of this book is available from the British Library.

Typeset, printed and bound by Rex Merchant @ Norman Cottage
Clown graphic by Roy Pack

THE PIED PUNCH AND JUDY MAN

The Runford Chronicles
Book Three.

By

Rex Merchant

Published by

Rex Merchant
@
Norman Cottage

*Dedicated to Erica for her love and tolerance
and to Nicola*

Chapter One.

"Be a good chap, Oswald. Don't spend all night down that cellar playing with your weather magic. Even high wizards need their sleep." Malcolm Gotobed walked over to the shop door, clicked the deadlock and turned the open sign to read, 'Closed - Even for the sale of Gotobed's Pile Ointment'. Getting no reaction to his comments, Malcolm tried again.

"Don't you forget it's market day tomorrow. I shall need your help in the shop all day." There was still no reply, but he could hear Oswald moving about in the cellar. Malcolm shook his head in despair. It was obvious that Oswald was choosing to ignore him. He wasn't surprised by it. Nothing altered. Oswald would never grow up. Even though they were now middle-aged men, his twin continued to act like some spoilt, overgrown schoolboy.

Malcolm emptied the till and counted the day's takings, sealing them in the night safe bag to deposit at the bank on his way home. Even while he was checking the money, his mind was still on his twin brother. When he'd done a trial balance, he walked to the top of the cellar steps and tried again.

"What you need is a wife. Someone to take your mind off these mad schemes. Why don't you ask Lydia Postlethwaite to marry you? Surely you and that barmaid have been friends for long enough to make a go of it?"

Minutes later, as he filled in the figures on the bank slip, Malcolm paused to glance around the office. He caught sight of his own wedding photograph, sitting in pride of place on the desk, surrounded by his other family snapshots. Those reminded him of his own fulfilled life; happily married to a wonderful wife, with a new baby daughter to bless their union. He was confident of his position in both town and church. He was a useful member of Runford society. Maybe he should feel pity for Oswald, living alone, spending his leisure time studying those ridiculous magic spells. Malcolm's attitude softened towards his brother. He had everything he could ever want out of life. Perhaps he had been a bit unchristian, criticising Oswald like that. Malcolm cast a professional eye over the sales area and the dispensary before he turned off the window lights to deter any late shoppers from rattling the door.

"Goodnight, Oswald. Don't work too late." He called over his shoulder as he let himself out of the pharmacy.

Oswald relaxed as the doorbell jangled noisily, confirming that Malcolm had at last left the premises. He hurried up the cellar stairs to check the shop door was securely locked.

"Thank God! He's gone at last. Freda had their baby, but I'm sure he's a candidate for the Mothers Union. Now perhaps I can get on with more important things." Still muttering to himself, he gathered a handful of equipment from the home brew shelves and hurried back to his underground laboratory in the shop's cellar.

'Gotobeds Brothers. Chemists and Druggists' was the only retail pharmacy in Runford. The business was owned and run by the Gotobed twins. The brothers were identical in appearance yet poles apart in temperament. Malcolm, known to all the locals as 'The Chemist', was the older of the two by a few hours, a fact he never forgot. He had reached the age when his figure and his bank balance had enlarged to comfortable proportions, but his curly hair was thinning and turning grey.

Oswald was a qualified pharmacist like his brother, but he insisted on being called by the obsolete title of druggist. Alchemist would have been a better description for him, as he had always been fascinated by the occult. Oswald was a bachelor, but not from choice. He had a healthy interest in the opposite sex but few of them would be bothered with him. Even his long-standing affair with Lydia Postlethwaite, the landlady of the Dog in a Doublet, was more off than on. It came as no surprise when he took on the office of High Wizard to the Runford Union of Fenland Slodgers. However, it did surprise his brother when Oswald started to take his fanciful title seriously and spent all his time pouring over obscure books on magic.

The High Wizard installed himself in his cellar workshop and opened his book on weather magic, thumbing through the pages to find his place. The idea of studying weather magic had first come to him when the pharmacy had an overstock of suntan lotions, after the summer turned unseasonably wet. The possibility of influencing the local climate became more inviting when the expensive umbrellas he had ordered for the autumn trade, failed to sell because that autumn was unusually dry. Finally, when a mild winter ensured there was no demand for hot water bottles, that made his mind up for him. Weather control had to be a better bet than stock control.

Malcolm was very tolerant. In theory, he could understand that the loss of business was a good enough reason for Oswald wishing he could control the local climate. He didn't for one minute think his brother could do anything about the weather, but he was gullible enough to believe the interest might keep Oswald busy and out of mischief. It might keep him away from the pub. But he hadn't expected the idea to become an all consuming obsession.

The druggist had his own agenda. His motives were always self centred. He realised the man who controlled the weather could hold the local farmers to ransom. Fine weather was always needed at harvest time when they gathered in the crops. Rain was needed in the spring to germinate the seeds. Frost helped break up the ploughed fields in the winter and ensured a good bed of fine soil for the spring sowing. The wrong weather conditions at any time of the year could cost the farmers a lot of money. Oswald reasoned that the power to control the climate would be worth a few hundred brace of pheasant and several sacks of free potatoes to the man that wielded it.

"Damn American magic lessons! They don't even use the Queen's English." Oswald grumbled aloud. When he had started his search for instructions he found that courses on weather magic were not plentiful. Even the Runford Union of Fenland Slodgers, a learned society founded in the 19th century to study the more neglected backwaters of knowledge, had no information on the subject in its large collection of rare occult books. For months Oswald had searched the shelves at the RUFS library. He had surfed the Internet, rifled through antiquarian bibliophile lists and scavenged car boot sales. He'd even spent a weekend scouring the bookshops at Hay on Wye.

It was a shop in Hay that had eventually tracked down a correspondence course for him, but he had to be satisfied with a second hand, dog-eared copy, they had obtained through the Exchange and Mart. Being an American publication, this course was far from ideal for the English climate, but, he reasoned, beggars can't be choosers. He turned over the yellowing pages and studied the instructions.

"No way! I am not gyrating about in feathers, dressed in buckskins and war paint. I definitely am not performing Red Indian rain dances! I'm sure there must be less energetic ways of raising a storm than doing a Sioux version of Rock Around The Clock!"

Oswald had problems with many of the American ingredients, being forced to adapt the list by making use of herbs grown in his own part of Lincolnshire, or substitutes he begged from the allotments, or bought cheaply from the pharmacy wholesaler and the local greengrocer. After weeks of frantic activity, his experiments had reached a critical stage. Now for the big question.; would the modified spell work?

"This evening I'm ready for a dry run. If you can have a dry run when you're rain making!" He laughed aloud at the pun. Oswald always talked to himself as he worked. It was a natural reaction to the tension he was feeling.

The Druggist ground the ingredients to a fine powder in the dispensary's largest earthenware mortar, before he put the mixture of dry constituents into the gallon demijohn, borrowed from the home brew department. One at a time, he added pure rainwater and several less wholesome liquids to this recipe then rammed a rubber bung firmly into the neck of the bottle. Swirling the container around to mix everything thoroughly, he recited the ancient Red Indian weather chant. Multicoloured bubbles began to form in the brew, like gas in a lively pint of Lydia's best bitter. They rose to the surface and broke, forming a deep froth. He replaced the bottle on the workbench and made some mysterious passes over it with his hands. These hand movements were not in the American tradition. He had culled them from books on the European school of witchcraft. Satisfied he had done everything he could to ensure the spell worked, he sat down on a stool by the bench, to watch and wait for results.

Oswald was not a man known for doing things by halves. Normally he jumped in feet first and regretted it afterwards, but as it had taken a lot of time and effort to get so far with his experiments, he decided to try the weather spell on a small scale. For once he would be prudent and make use of a gallon glass bottle, instead of the skies over Runford, for his first try at rainmaking.

"My little storm in a teacup," he christened the miniature effort.

Inside the gallon container, he had created his own microclimate where he could control the weather and learn how to handle his new magic powers on a manageable scale. It was the end of a busy day in the pharmacy. He was too occupied to call on Lydia for his usual pint and pie, so he brewed up some coffee over the Bunsen burner and munched a chocolate biscuit while he waited for the magical reaction to start.

"Bloody slow business this... Mother Nature could never catch a bus! A watched storm never brews... and the same goes for this damn coffee!" He grumbled impatiently to himself.

Gradually the atmosphere in the closed container grew more humid. Droplets of moisture began to condense on the cold sides of the bottle. Rivulets of water ran down the glass. Like trickles of perspiration down a navvy's rear cleavage, they coursed down the sides of the bottle to the bottom. At last, a single fluffy white cloud formed in the air space beneath the bottle neck. It was a perfect cumulus cloud in miniature, hovering above the mixture in the jar. Oswald rubbed his hands together in eager anticipation. Always the optimist, he let his imagination run riot.

"Success! I know this is only on a small scale, but large oaks from little acorns grow. This time a gallon jar, next time South Lincolnshire. Today a dribble, tomorrow hurricane Oswald! You might say the sky's the limit."

The Wizard poured a coffee and sipped it slowly as he watched with fatherly pride. The small white cloud darkened to deep grey, and began to shed tiny raindrops. There was even a small clap of thunder as a minute bright discharge of static electricity bounced around the inside of the bottle. He was so delighted with the results he jumped off his stool and jigged excitedly around the laboratory.

"Wonderful! I am a clever devil. No wonder I'm the High Wizard." Oswald danced around his experiment, grinning like the best man at a nudist wedding. Unfortunately, by pure accident, or maybe a Freudian slip, he chose to use some of the Rain Dance steps he had seen in the Red Indian weather-making course.

The cumulus cloud grew even darker, filling all the available space in the bottle. The small-scale storm gathered momentum. Lightning flashed every few seconds and the thunder reverberated around the underground laboratory, halting the dancer in his tracks. Oswald gasped at the sudden transformation and panicked. He grabbed the demijohn, lifted it from his workbench and rushed it to the far end of his laboratory, where the cellar ran under the pavement. He abandoned the erupting bottle on the floor, directly under the metal frame of thick, frosted glass tiles, set into a window in the pavement above, to allow daylight to filter down to the cellar. Oswald retreated quickly to the far end of his laboratory and stood at the bottom of the stairs, ready to make a quick getaway if things got out of hand.

The glass container shook visibly and the contents bubbled violently. A shaft of stray sunlight shone directly onto it, through a gap in the glass paving, where one of the tiles was broken. This warming sunlight accelerated the reaction, raising the temperature and increasing the pressure inside the bottle to bursting point. Oswald knew the experiment was out of control. He shielded his face with his hands, squinting between his fingers at the reaction, fearful in case the container burst and splinters of glass flew everywhere.

Luckily the seal in the neck broke first. The rubber bung shot out of the demijohn with the force of a puck at an ice hockey match. It hit the wall and ricocheted around the enclosed room with the speed of a rubber bullet, smashing the beaker of steaming coffee, as it skimmed along the bench top.

Oswald breathed a sigh of relief as the storm subsided and the froth in the bottle began to settle to the bottom. After a time he plucked up enough courage to approach the spent experiment, to verify it had indeed run its course. Like a man checking a dud firework, he leaned cautiously towards the bottle and peered at it. All seemed well. He relaxed. What if there had been a hairy moment or two? He shrugged his shoulders. Things may have been very tense for a few minutes but he had succeeded in raising a storm. He knew he was on the right path to controlling the weather and he felt pleased with himself. He swept all the broken pieces of glass and crockery from the bench and dumped them in the waste bin. But, deciding discretion was the best policy, he left the demijohn sitting on the floor under the glass-tiled pavement. Teething problems or not, he knew the experiment had served its purpose and proved he was on the right track. He mopped up the pool of coffee, happy with his results. Now the first attempt was over, he was sure nothing more could go wrong.

Unfortunately, the Wizard was wrong! A glance towards the sunlit end of his workshop would have shown him the experiment was far from over. He would have noticed the tiny storm cloud, unfettered now the bung had blown out, escape from the glass bottle and drift upwards to the ceiling. There it followed the flow of warm air through the break in the glass pavement and up into the freedom of the High Street.

The Wizard was oblivious to these events. Even if he had been aware of them he could have done nothing. Weaving weather spells is like swallowing laxatives - once set in motion they have a habit of working themselves through.

With the release of all that pent-up energy, and the escape of the storm cloud, the reaction in the gallon jar quickly subsided, allowing the wizard to finish clearing up the mess. He whistled cheerfully as he mopped up the dregs and rinsed out the demijohn, before replacing it on the sales shelves in the shop. He convinced himself it had all gone to plan. He was confident he would be able to reproduce his results in the open air, but on a much larger scale.

"Eat your heart out, you TV weather forecasters," he chortled happily. "You and your satellites can only observe the weather. I can make it happen."

Oswald's faith in his rain making abilities was well founded. The escaped cloud rose above the pavement at the front of the chemist shop. As it ascended, it grew bigger. It floated gently over the market place and was eventually sucked into the space above the Hole-in-the-Wall passageway. There the high walls and tall buildings formed a funnel, fostering a natural flow of air.

The mini storm finally came to rest over the oldest part of the passage wall, a fragile section built of ancient sandstone. It started to rain over that small area. The cloud shuddered visibly and discharged its static charge. A loud clap of thunder rent the air. A single bolt of lightning struck the old stonework, splitting it to the foundations.

While this was happening, Oswald was already leaving the shop and walking in the opposite direction, making for the Dog in a Doublet for a celebratory drink. If he had been using the Hole-in–the–Wall passage at that quiet time of an evening he would have been dismayed at the force of that brief storm and shocked at the damaged he had caused to the ancient wall.

Chapter Two

"Is he dead, Mr Willis? Honestly he wasn't in that state when I went to fetch you." How could Michael have got himself into such a fix? Cuthbert Stothard, the council foreman, thought glumly. His labourer must have returned to the site, opened up more of the wall and somehow got stuck in a recess inside it. He shook his head. It just didn't make sense. Michael Flannegan never lifted a finger without first being told what to do by his gaffer. Damn it! Cuthbert knew from experience, the labourer always needed to be told everything at least three times.

"His eyes are open. I'm sure he's breathing. Help me get him out of there, then we'll see what's happened to him." Theo Willis took charge of the situation. In spite of his portly figure he clambered over the mound of fallen masonry and peered in at the still figure of the Irishman.

Cuthbert rushed to help. Between them they lifted Michael clear of the stone recess and out into the open, supporting his rigid body by the ankles and head, as if he was a scaffold plank.

"Easy does it, Michael. Mr Willis and I have got you now." Cuthbert did his best to reassure the casualty as they lowered his stiff form onto the pavement.

Theo stood back to regain his breath, then bent over to examine the patient. "Good Lord! It's just like tetanus!" He straightened up in astonishment, then noticing the puzzled expression on Cuthbert's face, he explained.

"He's rigid! He's stiff! All his muscles seem to be in spasm." He examined the Irishman again.

"There's a strong pulse and he's breathing, but it's very shallow." Theo stood upright and mopped his brow, where beads of sweat had formed from his unaccustomed exertions. As he brushed himself down with his handkerchief, clouds of sandstone dust rose from his baggy business suit.

"Oh dear! Oh dear! There's Michael at death's door and you in a mess. What am I going to do? Tell me, what am I going to do?" Cuthbert buzzed around Theo and the casualty like a demented bluebottle. The council foreman was having a bad day. He didn't like surprises.

"Don't worry about me, I'll clean up. It's Michael you should be concerned about. Just run to the chemists and ring for an ambulance. Tell them Michael has had some sort of seizure."

As he hurried across the marketplace to Gotobeds Pharmacy, which was the nearest shop with a telephone, Cuthbert had tried to make sense of the events that led to the disaster. He and Michael had been asked to repair the old wall in the Hole-in-the-Wall passage where some of the masonry had fallen down during the night. An early morning paperboy had complained he couldn't get through to complete his round. It was a mystery to the council why the wall should have crumbled. Their surveyor had checked it only weeks before and pronounced it sound. The dressed outer stones had come away leaving the rubble filling in a dangerous state.

When Cuthbert and Michael pulled out this loose filling, they found something totally unexpected. Set in the rubble was a doorway, outlined in dressed stones. It was a perfect Norman arch, about seven feet high, and in an excellent state of preservation.

"That must have been covered over soon after it was built. Apart from the dust, it looks as if it was built yesterday." The builder ran his expert fingers over the smooth surface of the dressed stones then checked the state of the rubble that filled in the space under the arch.

"Looks as if they made a mistake building the

doorway here and decided to fill it in immediately." He took out a large spotted handkerchief and flapped the area. Clouds of dust, the accumulation of centuries, engulfed him, making him cough and splutter. When the dust cleared away, another intriguing sight met his eyes. Across the centre of the arch hung an old rope, bearing a saucer like wax disk. It was all smothered in cobwebs, looking as if it had not been disturbed for ages.

Cuthbert knew he was out of his depth. He downed tools and decided to call in an expert. Theo Willis, the antique dealer and keen local historian, was the man everyone turned to on such occasions. Theo was always interested in any historical finds. He was always reminding people to let him know if anything unusual turned up when they were digging their allotments or knocking down their old buildings.

"We'll not disturb this any more, Michael. I'll go and get Mr Willis to take a look at it. He'll be opening his antique shop by this time of the morning."

"Right you are, Gaffer. I'll away to the cafe and fetch a couple of bacon sandwiches. We've been at work all of twenty minutes. I'm thinking it must be time for our first tea break, to be sure."

That was how Cuthbert had left things. Everything appeared to be under control. He couldn't understand what had gone wrong. When he had returned with Theo Willis they found Michael Flannegan unconscious and partly encased in the wall. Even though he had no idea what had happened, Cuthbert felt responsible. He dashed across the market place to ring for an ambulance.

Five minutes later the foreman hurried back from making his emergency phonecall, followed closely by the druggist, Oswald Gotobed, who had overheard the telephone conversation and thought he may be needed to give Michael some first aid. Happily their worst fears were unfounded. They found Michael sitting up against the wall, looking perfectly healthy. Granted, he had a stupid smile on his face and a faraway expression in his eyes, but that was nothing new. It was the way he always looked at pub closing time.

When he arrived back at the scene of the accident, Cuthbert was even more surprised to hear the Irishman mumbling tunefully, singing a song he often performed at the Dog in a Doublet, as the evening's drinking drew to a close.

"When Irish eyes are smiling...sure it's like the..."

Oswald leaned over the patient to smell his breath. "He's not drunk again, is he? It's a bit early in the day, even for him."

Theo shook his head and dismissed the

suggestion.

"No. I checked whether he was sober when he came round. Michael seems quite normal to me. He's just a bit dazed." Having dismissed the labourer's condition as trivial, Theo turned excitedly to the arch in the wall.

"But just you come over here and look at this. I'm fascinated. It's some kind of saucer shaped disc."

"I can't waste time chatting to you, " Oswald growled. "I was in the middle of the morning dispensing rush when Cuthbert interrupted me. I'm going back to the shop." He stalked off across the market place in a huff, upset that Theo had everything in hand and his own first-aid knowledge was not required. He didn't like other people wasting his time. He preferred to do that for himself.

Seeing the hurt expression on Theo's face at Oswald's off hand manner, Cuthbert enquired solicitously. "Let me see. What have you found? Could it be worth anything?"

Theo showed the wax disc to the council foreman, then put it quickly into his pocket. Since talking to Oswald, he'd had time to realise it might be valuable and he could sell it through his antique shop. He had no intention of sharing the windfall with Cuthbert or his employers.

"Could be a seal, like you see on those old

charters." Cuthbert suggested.

Theo didn't reply. He had already worked out that much, for himself. He turned his back on the foreman and surreptitiously retrieved the wax disc from his pocket. He peered at the uneven surface through his pocket magnifier, unable to resist another look, like a pubescent schoolboy examining his first nude centrefold.

"What do you make of all this?" Cuthbert cast his expert eye over the damaged wall and spread his hands in a gesture of helplessness.

Theo shook his head in wonder at his lucky find. It took him several seconds before Cuthbert's question registered through his euphoria, then he misunderstood the remark, and treated Cuthbert to his views on the historical significance of the seal.

"This wax seal appears to bear the badge of one of the old priors of Runford and there are some mysterious archaic symbols impressed into the other side. It's very old, possibly even medieval. I'm convinced this small section of the wall was part of the old Runford priory. I'll know more when I've taken the seal across to the RUFS library to examine it properly."

Cuthbert felt that was all irrelevant compared with his problems, but he didn't dare say so. He seized on Theo's last comment and sniffed disapprovingly. "Oh yes...you're a member of the RUFS, aren't you." Then he added under his breath. "They're a funny lot, them RUFS."

Theo looked up sharply at the comment and frowned.

Cuthbert, realising he may have spoken out of turn, hastily went on to change the subject. "Begging your pardon. When I asked what you made of it all, I didn't mean the disc, I meant this queer business with Michael and the damage to the wall."

Theo was about to give his medical opinion on the Irishman's condition, when he was distracted by something he saw pushed into a corner of the sandstone recess.

"Ah! What's this then?" He bent over and prised out a small grimy object and held it up.

"It's a child's rattle," Cuthbert suggested.

"No, it's too big." Theo turned his new find over in his hand. His face broke into a smile of recognition. "It's a jester's stick! Look, here are the remains of a bell and a faded ribbon." He held up the thin piece of wood to show the attachments. "That dried up piece of leather tied to the base, could well be the remains of a pig's bladder."

They went no further with their investigations because they were interrupted by the wail of an ambulance siren. The vehicle screeched to a halt in the marketplace. The crew jumped out and rushed down the Hole-in-the–Wall passageway, their urgent footsteps clattering noisily on the York slabs.

Theo stuffed the jester's toy into his jacket pocket beside the wax seal and followed Cuthbert and the paramedics. They watched the crew load Michael into the back of the ambulance, securely strapped onto a stretcher. He was still happily humming the strains of his favourite Irish melody.

The rescue vehicle left the marketplace, emergency siren blaring and blue lights flashing, as it raced to the Runford Cottage Hospital.

Theo returned his attention to his recent finds. "I'm astonished at what I've found. Frankly, I am amazed!" He gently patted the bulge in his jacket pocket, took out the wax seal, and was about to bore Cuthbert even more with his ideas on his new toys, when the sound of unexpected movement made them both turn back to the deserted passageway.

"Who the devil's that?" Theo frowned. A tall man in a dirty black and white suit, ducked clumsily under the council barrier. The man adjusted his peculiar three-pointed hat, brushing a layer of thick dust from the top of it, and stepped into the marketplace.

"Top of the morning to you, gaffers." The newcomer greeted Cuthbert and Theo like an old friend, addressing them in an Irish voice, which sounded exactly like that of Michael Flannegan.

Theo was still holding the seal in his hand when he turned to look at the new arrival. The man hesitated, looked at the seal and then turned his full attention onto the antique dealer. Their eyes met. An involuntary shudder ran through Theo's body. He felt suddenly and unaccountably fearful as the stranger's gaze bore into his mind. The feeling was over almost as soon as it had begun. The man smiled and turned to walk away.

The foreman scratched his head and stared after the retreating figure. Angrily, he exclaimed. "Did you see that? Some people take no notice of 'No Entry' sign. He had no business being in there...What do you make of that daft costume? Bit of a tight fit, isn't it? It's stretched over his body like the skin of a Lincolnshire sausage...especially that enlarged bit at the front!"

"Looked like a clown's suit or a court jester's outfit to me. By the way, 'that bit at the front' as you call it, was fashionable in Europe in the middle ages. It's called a codpiece."

"Codpiece! More like a Whalepiece in his case. I think I've heard them called a braggart. I bet he's pushed a cucumber in there so that he can brag about it"

Theo ignored the comments on the clown's

ample manhood. "Perhaps he's here for the fete at the weekend?"

Cuthbert stared hard after the gaunt figure and muttered uneasily to himself. "He called me gaffer, just like Michael does. How the hell does he know who I am? I've never set eyes on him before in my life." He watched the peculiar stranger limp stiffly across the marketplace until he was out of sight. With a shrug, Cuthbert put his irritation aside and returned his thoughts to the injured labourer.

"I do hope Michael's going to be alright. Apart from being bone idle and drinking too much, he's not a bad lad really."

Chapter Three

Strapped securely onto a stretcher, Michael Flannegan stared up at the roof of the speeding ambulance and mused happily on the morning's events that had landed him in need of medical attention.

He remembered he had gone to buy the bacon sandwiches for their lunch break and had made an unauthorised stop on his way. The errand had taken rather longer than he had anticipated. He recalled being worried about his long absence and he remembered rehearsing excuses as he hurried back to the building site in the passage.

"I'm sorry it took me ages to fetch the sandwiches, gaffer, but I had to give the kiss of death to an old lady in the bookies!... No! No! Kiss of death doesn't sound quite right! No! No! Mustn't mention the bookmakers!" He had another think.

"I ran across Father Flynn in the bookmakers. He enquired why I hadn't been to mass last Sunday, as I usually do...No! No! That won't do!"

Recalling his intentions to take Father Flynn's name in vain, Michael disentangled his arms from the stretcher harness and crossed himself religiously at the thought of all those blasphemous lies he had intended to use. He had not met the priest that morning and he had not attended church for years.

When he had finally returned, breathless at the work site in the passageway, he started to offer the apologies he'd invented before he realised that his gaffer was not there.

"Sorry I'm late, gaffer, but there was Father Flynn and this old lady...Well I'll be a Donegal donkey! I can see he's nowhere to be seen. He's gone missing and he's not back yet."

Finding himself unexpectedly alone, Michael unwrapped the food, put the smaller bacon roll into the foreman's bag and sat down to eat the larger one.

The passageway was deserted, thanks to the No Entry signs they had erected at each end of it. The warmth of the morning sun made him feel quite drowsy. The previous evening he had enjoyed a good night out with the lads at the Dog in a Doublet. The pub's darts team always performed better when they were well tanked up. They found it much easier to score with two boards to aim at. Unfortunately the soporific effect of the beer always carried over to the morning after.

Michael was licking his fingers and regretting he had not bought himself two of the bacon rolls, when he was disturbed by the sound of falling masonry. He had glanced up apprehensively.

"Surely to goodness! Is it all going to fall down now?" The question froze on his lips as the dusty figure of a tall thin man stepped out of the cloud of dust and onto the pavement beside him. The stranger wiped the thick covering of dirt and cobwebs from his face, smiled broadly and turned to face the amazed Irishman.

Michael remembered the man's eyes lighting up. He guessed it wasn't just because the fellow was pleased to see him, because the eyes literally glowed and lit up with an arresting inner light. Michael returned the smile then panicked as he found it impossible to look away. Gradually his fear retreated as the eyes grew brighter. It was as compelling viewing as Coronation Street. As surely as a rabbit eyeballing a hungry stoat, Michael found himself transfixed by that hypnotic stare.

The next thing Michael remembered was the distant sound of music. He found himself looking into the laughing, green eyes of his long dead mother. Irish pipes were playing the familiar strains of 'When Irish eyes are smiling'. The lilting melody filled the air around him. Michael's body had stiffened. He sat bolt upright. The mug of tea fell from his numb fingers as his eyes clouded over with tears of joy. The two figures stayed immobile, the clown staring intensely down at the labourer and Michael smiling serenely up into the dusty face. For once the glazed expression on Michael's face owed nothing to the amount of the Guinness he had consumed the previous night, for his muscles were rigid, lacking the relaxed tone of drunkenness. His limbs moved involuntarily, twitching at random like a victim of the electric chair.

Michael gulped in surprise as the man's eyes took on a deeper glow. It felt as if the stranger actually entered his head through the windows of his eyes and searched through his mind, like a burglar rifling through his personal belongings. Every thought and memory Michael had ever experienced, flashed before him like a drowning man going down for the third time. Strangely, he felt no panic. The experience seemed distant and no real concern of his. He felt detached. There was nothing of the outrage he should have experienced from such a violation. Fleetingly, among the jumble of memories, he recalled some good advice he had heard from his older sister when one of the nuns had taught her the facts of life.

"If rape becomes inevitable, my dear, just lie back and enjoy it."

Michael did just that until the paramedics came for him.

As the ambulance skidded to a halt outside the casualty department at the hospital,　Michael regained consciousness. He stopped singing, raised his head from the pillow and asked the medic at his side. "Jesus!　Did I doze off and imagine it all? Where did that nice clown go to?"

Chapter Four

The tall stranger in the black and white clown outfit, stalked across the marketplace. He ignored the curious glances and sniggers of a group of Grammar School boys, who were skulking in Barclays Bank doorway, eating fish and chips from page three of the newspaper, when they should have been studying in the school library. He speeded up when Tina Stothard led her class of juniors across the square towards the library. They waved at him, delighted to see a clown in the street. He didn't return their greetings, preferring to answer the children with a scowl.

Even though he was a stranger, the clown seemed to know exactly where he was going. He strode purposefully into Gotobeds Chemist shop as if he had been shopping there many times before.

Malcolm Gotobed stood behind the shop counter, dusting and rearranging bottles of tablets and packets of cough lozenges.

Oswald Gotobed was busy in the dispensary,

weighing out powders and measuring potions for his latest occult experiments, which he intended to conduct after hours, below stairs in his private laboratory. As he worked, he was dreaming of a steamy session with Lydia Postlethwait, the landlady of his local pub, if he could only worm his way into her good books again.

Peeved at being the only one doing any useful work, Malcolm aired some of his complaints against his brother. "I don't know why you waste so much time fiddling with your so-called, magic spells, and all that stuff and nonsense you practise at the RUFS. Controlling the weather, I ask you! I don't know how you've the nerve to believe such stuff and to call yourself a High Wizard. You don't give a jot what effect it will have on our business. Our customers will think you're unbalanced. I'm surprised they still trust you to dispense their prescriptions."

"I waste nothing like the time you spend at that church, playing the organ, chatting up the vicar and conducting choir practice. You spend more hours kneeling down, wearing out your trouser knees, in the company of a man in a dress, than I ever do at the RUFS. You're always going on about Virgin Births and Holy Ghosts. And what about that turning water to wine bit? You've got a nerve, calling my beliefs rubbish!" Oswald answered, over the top of the polished mahogany dispensary screen. By standing on his tiptoes he could just see his brother between the glass carboys of coloured water adorning the top shelf. He glanced up from the weighing scales to see if his sarcastic answer had hit the mark.

The familiar ring of the shop doorbell announced the arrival of another customer. From the privacy of the dispensary, Oswald was only vaguely aware of what was happening in the shop as he got on with his weighing and measuring. He listened with only half an ear to this latest transaction.

A melodious Irish voice, which Oswald recognised instantly as Michael Flannegan's, greeted Malcolm cheerily. "Top of the morning to you, sir, to be sure."

"What can I get you?"

"I require some money. I think I'll have two twenty pound notes from the till, if you please. It's to pay for me board and lodgings, you'll understand."

Oswald smiled to himself. Michael was obviously non the worse for his accident. Joking requests for money were a favourite line of banter with many of the regulars. He had heard it all before. He ran over the routine in his mind.

"What would you like?" The shop assistant would ask.

"A pound out of the till." The hopeful customer

would snigger and the assistant would laugh as if he appreciated the joke.

The patter always ran along those lines. But it had lost its novelty after the first few hundred repeats.

Suddenly the Druggist's ears pricked up. The routine was not going along as usual. This was no longer a silly joke! The tinkle of the 'no sale' bell on the till, sounded across the shop. Peering out from behind the carboys he saw Malcolm was holding out two twenty-pound notes to the customer. At a glance he could see it definitely wasn't Michael Flannegan standing there, but some strangely dressed chap he'd never set eyes on before.

"What the devil's going on here?" Oswald rushed from the dispensary and confronted the two men. He was surprised to find Malcolm standing rigidly to attention at the open till, a faraway look in his eyes and a blank expression on his face. That was completely out of character, for Malcolm always took an interest in his customers, smiling at them as if they were old friends. Oswald also noticed his brother's hands were moving jerkily like a robotic dancer, as he passed the money over to the waiting customer.

The Druggist snatched the notes from his brother's fingers before he could give them away. He turned to glare accusingly at the stranger, expecting the man to make a dash for the door, but he came face to face with a nightmare. Oswald found himself glaring into a pair of gleaming green eyes, which returned his challenging stare with the intensity of laser beams. The Wizard swallowed hard but didn't lose his nerve. If the fellow wanted a staring match he could have one. Drawing on the hundreds of hours of occult training he had undertaken to attain the highest grade of adept in the RUFS, he fought off the mental challenge. He tried to turn the tables on his adversary by seeing into the mind of his opponent. The two men faced up to each other over the chemist counter. Neither of them blinked an eyelid. They were like two gunfighters from the old West, challenging each other to be the first to back down and look away.

For once the High Wizard met his match. The stranger's mind did not respond as he expected. It was like no other he had ever come across. Oswald could make no sense of the man's mind. He might as well have tried to read a floppy disk without a computer, or decipher a locum doctor's prescriptions without his reading glasses.

Abruptly the contest ceased. The green eyes lost their glow. The stranger smiled disarmingly, bowed low and touched his jester's cap, giving a touch of old fashioned charm to his farewell. He turned away without a word of apology and limped out of the shop.

Oswald stared after the clown and frowned in disbelief. No one had ever engaged his mind like that. He knew he hadn't overcome the man in their mental contest. It was as if a truce had been called until they met again. He scratched his head and pondered. Who was this stranger? Where had he received such expert training in the esoteric arts?

Malcolm shook himself like a man awaking from a dream and carried on with his dusting as if nothing had happened

"What was going on there? Why were you giving that fellow our hard earned takings?" Oswald asked testily. "I know you believe in giving freely to the church and to your good causes, but fancy handing over forty quid just because some thieving fool asked you for it. You have a go at me for not pulling my weight, but you give the profits away. Don't you ever forget, brother, charity begins at home."

"What fellow? What charity?" Malcolm looked vacantly about the empty shop, searching for whoever the fellow might be and trying to make sense of his brother's accusations.

"Oh forget it!" Oswald grunted wearily, as the shop door jangled open again and an attractive young lady came in. He had more important things to think about than itinerant clowns with the knack of hypnosis. Serving Cuthbert Stothard's attractive daughter was definitely one of them.

"Ah, Tina! What can we do for you? Do you need some first aid stuff for the school or the Brownies, or has your dad run out of indigestion mixture again?"

"No. I bought him a large bottle only last week. I've not come to see you about business. I was hoping you could display a poster for me. It's advertising a meeting of the Runford Natural History Society."

Oswald took the poster from her, unrolled it and read the announcement aloud.

"A lecture on the Black Panther of Dartmoor.' That should be interesting, Tina. How come you've been landed with the job of distributing these?"

"I've taken on the position of mammal recorder for the society. Will you and your brother come to the meeting?"

"I'm sure Malcolm will. He's a keen naturalist." Oswald walked around the counter to get a better view of the girl. He licked his lips as he ogled Tina's slim figure.

"Maybe it's time I developed an interest in nature. Looking at you...I mean seeing how interested you are in the subject, I certainly feel it's a distinct possibility. I'll personally see to it that your announcement gets the best position in our window."

Chapter Five

Theo Willis left the marketplace soon after the ambulance had taken Michael Flannegan to the hospital. Instead of returning to his antique shop, he went straight to the old Working Men's Institute building, where the Runford Union of Fenland Slodgers held their meetings. On the upper floor of this establishment, the RUFS housed a vast library of specialist books. Theo was honorary librarian to the Society. He had taken over the job from Oswald Gotobed, who never had carried out the duties properly as he was far too busy playing High Wizard to the group.

Theo didn't hold with all that esoteric magic nonsense but he did appreciate the contents of the library, for in the many years of its existence the RUFS had amassed a unique collection of books, including an enviable section on local history. Everything ever published, privately or publicly, on the history of the Lincolnshire fens, was to be found on the society's bookshelves. Theo loved local history and was in his element. He spent several days each week happily cataloguing and researching these volumes, leaving his wife to look after their antique business. Reverently, he placed the seal on the library table and positioned a magnifying glass above it. For a start, he intended to check the prior's imprint in the wax surface, to try and date it.

In spite of the age of the seal, the image was still clearly visible as a tonsured figure at prayer, kneeling before a cross, surrounded by numerous smaller monks. He checked through the illustrations of priory seals on various deeds and documents, until he confirmed that this example was the seal of William d' Angier, who had been prior at Runford during the first half of the fifteenth century. Theo grinned smugly to himself at his success and turned the seal over to study the other side.

The reverse of the wax seal proved much more difficult to understand. Theo spent many fruitless hours pouring over the official records trying to decipher its meaning. Finally he gave up in despair, reluctantly deciding he had no choice but to contact his predecessor. As a last resort he telephoned Oswald Gotobed to ask if he would come to inspect the seal and maybe shed some light on the strange hieroglyphics.

At the close of business, Oswald left his brother to balance the day's takings and lock up the shop, while he crossed the road to the chip shop to collect his tea. As a bachelor living alone, he rarely bothered to cook. He existed on fish, chips and coffee, a monotonous diet broken occasional by a more substantial meal at the Dog in a Doublet, when he could persuade the landlady to cook for him. He had been known to enjoy Lydia's hot dinners and stay over for breakfast, but that was a thing of the past. He had upset her once too often and she had dumped him.

That evening he collected his meal from the chip shop, wrapped up in the pink pages of the Financial Times, a favour the owner of the shop reserved for his more discerning business customers.

"I see you've let the flat above the shop." The Druggist commented, as he shook the vinegar bottle over his chips and cod.

"Ah yes! I've let it to a young lady by the name of Mavis Peabody. She works as an usherette at the cinema." As he spoke, he checked the chips that were simmering in the pan, nipping the odd one between his fingers to feel if it was cooked.

"Ah! Are you referring to The Miss Mavis Peabody, the local tart? With her in residence, you'll have to change the side light from white to red."

Oswald sniggered. "How come you were persuaded to let her rent your flat? She might get your shop a bad name. Then again, she might well bring the punters in. Half an hour's workout, upstairs with Mavis, and they'll work up enough of an appetite to come down here and eat like horses!"

"I couldn't refuse her offer. She has influential friends. Some anonymous person has paid her deposit and her rent in cash, in advance. Several upstanding local citizens have given her glowing references." The fryer tapped the side of his shiny nose with a greasy forefinger to advise discretion. "I can't say too much, but a nod's as good as a wink to a blind donkey. She and her customers won't be bothered by the local police, that's for sure!"

Oswald, still pondering on those cryptic remarks, crossed the road and let himself into the Union building.

Upstairs in the library, Theo Willis was still struggling with the translation of the wax seal. He had every available book on the medieval history of the Runford priory spread out on the table around him. There were numerous pieces of paper peeping out from between the pages, keeping relevant references to hand.

"Evening, Theo. I can spare you just half an hour, then I must get on with my invisibility spells and

40

some weather magic. I take it you've had no luck yet?" Oswald greeted the librarian briskly, recalling with relish the pleading phonecall he'd received during the afternoon rush of prescriptions.

"No, nothing. I've drawn a complete blank. I doubt if you can help, but I thought I'd better ask."

"Perhaps you're looking in the wrong place." Oswald chose to ignore the librarian for the minute and sauntered over to the shelf of grimoires. "I had an idea today about my shoes." He looked over his glasses at Theo, but got no reaction to his comment. This was no surprise, as Theo had no idea about the problem with Oswald's feet.

The Wizard had perfected the art of making himself invisible but when he recited the usual spell, his shoes and socks stubbornly refused to vanish. They remained completely and embarrassingly visible. Oswald had given the problem much thought and had taken professional advice. He now understood why it was happening. He knew he had a mental block about his feet because he was embarrassed with their ugly bunions and corns. The thought of removing his shoes and socks in public, even metaphorically by magic, was too much for his subconscious to allow. However, knowing the reason for his failure had not helped him solve the problem. If he wanted to be completely undetectable when he went invisible, he still had to remove his shoes and socks first. That meant he had to be very careful where he trod.

Oswald continued. "You know I can go invisible, but my shoes always stay in view. Well I've decided to make them invisible first, then see to the rest of me. It's as simple as that. I don't know why I didn't think of it before." To demonstrate his prowess, he recited a spell under his breath and made a magic pass at his feet. His shoes, socks and feet vanished, leaving him looking like a man chopped off at the ankles.

"Terrific! That has solved my problem. Easy when you think about it." Oswald gloated.

Theo glanced up at the Wizard, saw he appeared to have no feet and assumed he'd used mirrors to conceal them.He rolled his eyes towards the ceiling and asked pointedly. "Now you've had your fun, do you have time to spare to look at this wax seal?"

Oswald reversed the spell, sauntered from the bookshelves to the library table and glanced casually over the librarian's shoulder at the wax disc. What he saw made him choke on his chips. All thoughts of disappearing feet and conjuring up sunshine and showers were driven straight out of his mind.

"That is bloody amazing! I've never seen one in the flesh before. Wherever did you get it?"

"Ah! Now you see why I was so interested. It is

an ancient priory seal and it has the imprint of William d'Angier on the reverse."

"Damn the reverse! Look at the obverse! That's a potent medieval magic spell impressed in that disk. That is very rare indeed. That is absolutely fascinating."

Theo sat back in his chair with a grunt of disbelief and peered over his reading glasses at his visitor.

"You think you've recognised it already? One glance and you can declare it's a magic spell? I might have expected that explanation from the High blooming Wizard! Are you sure you're not guessing?"

Oswald was already climbing the library steps to the very top shelf where they stored the rare grimoires and treatises on ancient magic. Cold greasy chips rained down as the excited Druggist struggled with his dinner in one hand and balanced an old, leather-bound volume in the other. Dust off the vellum pages drifted down like finely ground pepper onto the fallen chips. He slid down the handrail, riding it like a schoolboy on a banister. "I just knew it! It's identical to one I've seen in here," he shouted triumphantly.

Theo brushed a cold chip from his shoulder and looked very peeved. Trust the High flipping Wizard to put his finger straight on the solution to the mystery! He had spent all day looking in the wrong place for the answers and that idiot had found it immediately. Life could be very cruel.

"Beginner's luck," he muttered under his breath.

Oswald placed the open book beside the wax disk on the desk and compared it in minute detail. Sure enough, the old wood cut illustration matched the hieroglyphics exactly.

Theo took out his magnifying glass and insisted on checking every detail for himself. Finally he straightened up from the desk and had to admit that Oswald had solved the problem.

"What do you make of it, then?" He asked in a crestfallen voice.

"It's as clear as day," Oswald chortled. "It's a restraining spell. It was made to imprison someone, or something, so that they, or it, would never escape. It's a bit like the cork in the neck of the bottle, where the genie was trapped in the Tales from the Arabian Nights. You could even use it to keep your valuables safe. Something similar to the lock on a chastity belt! Now do tell me exactly where you found it?"

Theo took out his magnifying glass and once again compared the wax seal with the illustration in the book, in tight-lipped silence, hoping to find some discrepancy. Grudgingly he was forced to admit the High Wizard had solved the mystery. Eventually, as he could find no shadow of doubt, he sat back and explained the events of that morning at the Hole-in-the-Wall passage.

Oswald gulped down his chips and listened to the whole story. At the end of the tale, when his companion looked over to him for some favourable comment, the Wizard observed.

"Gives a whole new slant to the name 'Hole-in-the-Wall, doesn't it? I always believed the local tradition about the monks placing food in an alcove for the lepers: Ssmething like the off-sales hatch at the Dog in a Doublet. Now I am wondering if folk memory was actually referring to this mysterious chamber you've discovered inside the very fabric of the old stone wall."

"Good point that," Theo conceded grudgingly, wondering why he hadn't thought of it first.

"I'm wondering what was so valuable to prior William that he found it necessary to use such a potent talisman. There might be a priceless treasure hidden in that wall." Oswald said almost to himself, as he picked the last few pieces of vinegar soaked batter from the corners of the chip packet.

"You ask what was hidden in the wall? I found this jester's stick." Theo took the dusty remains from his pocket and spread them on the table.

Oswald peered at the bits of debris. "Hardly worth the trouble, was it?" He screwed up his greasy chip paper into a ball, tossed it expertly into the furthest waste paper bin, and changed the subject. "That pied Irish clown you saw coming out of the passageway. He came into our shop and tried to rob my brother of two twenty-pound notes. He needs watching if he's staying locally. Perhaps you could mention him to your brother George, the Chief Constable, next time you get an invite to the Manor House for tea."

"I'll do that. Any idea who the clown could be, or what he's doing in Runford?"

"I suppose he could be here for the fete at the weekend. The fete committee has all sorts of entertainment booked for the day...Mind you...I don't recall Malcolm saying the vicar had engaged any clowns. Come to think of it, I don't remember seeing clowns mentioned anywhere on the poster we fixed to the shop window." Oswald thought back to the conversation with the clown in the chemist shop. There had been some mention of wanting money for his board and lodgings. Almost to himself he asked. "I wonder where the cheeky blighter is staying?"

Chapter Six

Lydia Postlethwaite, the landlady of the Dog in a Doublet, leaned motionless on the bar, frozen in time like a still figure in a waxwork. Both her hands were poised in the act of polishing a pint glass. Her ample breasts rested on the mahogany counter top as she stared lovingly into the green eyes of the only customer in the bar. Her attention was concentrated solely on a clown in a close fitting, black and white outfit.

"Of course I have a room. You can have it free of charge. It will be a pleasure to put you up, for as long as you like, Mr er. . .?" She spoke in a mindless monotone, not at all like her usual animated self.

"My name is Mr Piper. You can call me Peter, if you like." The green glow in the customer's eyes died down.

The landlady resumed polishing the glasses as if nothing untoward had happened. She asked. "Would you care for a beer, on the house of course, while I make your room ready?"

"No thank you, Mrs Postlethwaite."

"Oh! Do call me Lydia." She flapped her false eyelashes at him like a lovesick schoolgirl at a pop concert and eased down the lace top of her boat neck blouse, just enough to reveal the very top of her tattoo, peeping coyly from the valley of her cleavage.

"I don't drink."

"Well what about some dinner, then? I've some nice rainbow trout in the oven or there's some cold pheasant pie in the fridge. We always use local grown produce."

"I don't eat, either."

"Well surely I can do something for you?" she asked suggestively, wriggling her bare shoulders to reveal a lot more of her tattoo.

"I am having trouble with my knee joints. Perhaps you have an oil can?"

Lydia hesitated at this strange request and stared at her guest. Convinced she saw a glimmer of a smile on his face, she chuckled to herself.

"You've got a wicked sense of humour, Mr Piper. I like a man who enjoys a good laugh."

At this point, Oswald and Theo called into the pub on their way home. Theo was full of his own importance and still expounding on the origins of the wax seal.

"Fancy me finding it intact after all these years. It's definitely a medieval seal "

"It's definitely a magic talisman. I was the one who found the reference to it, remember? Don't you forget, you were having no success even though you'd been struggling with it all afternoon. I think you owe me a drink for that information."

"Give us two pints of best bitter please, Lydia," Theo sighed wearily, pulling his purse from his inside pocket.

Oswald nudged him in the ribs as they walked over to the corner table and whispered out of the corner of his mouth. "See that clown at the bar. That's the blighter who was in our shop trying to rob the till this morning. He thought he could talk Malcolm out of forty quid. He put my brother into a trance and asked him for some cash from the till. Good job I was listening. I stepped in and foiled his plans, before he could get the money in his hands."

"A trance? Do you mean hypnosis?" The antique dealer asked incredulously.

"Something like that. It must have been. Can't be any other explanation."

Theo frowned and took a good look at the stranger.

"Did you get the police to sort him out?"

"No. He didn't actually get around to

committing a crime."

"Well I never! I'd better warn the wife." Theo eyed the stranger over the edge of his pint glass, and couldn't help noticing the doting looks the landlady was giving her new guest. "It would appear Lydia likes him, all the same."

Oswald scowled into his beer. He fancied Lydia himself. He had been working on their relationship for years, with mixed success. This was one more good reason to dislike that damn clown!

"If you will show me to my room, I would like to have a shower and freshen up a bit," the clown asked the landlady politely.

"Keep an eye on the bar for me, Oswald. I must just show Mr Peter Piper to his room." Lydia beamed at her new guest and led him from the bar into the private part of the house.

Oswald scowled after them but dutifully left his corner seat and walked to the counter to await any customers.

"Peter bloody Piper!" He grunted at Theo. "That's a made up name, if ever I heard one! Every school kid's heard of the idiot who picked a peck of pickled pepper. That must be his stage name, surely? With that costume and name, maybe he thinks he's the Pied Piper as well. Come to think of it, that oversized bulge in his codpiece could be where he hides his damn flute!" Oswald pulled himself a free pint of beer and sat on the stool behind the bar. It was a good twenty minutes before Lydia returned.

"You've taken your time!" Oswald grunted angrily.

Lydia ignored his aggressive tone and glanced around the room. "What's your problem? There's been no rush. You coped, surely?"

"That's not the point, Lydia. I might have been rushed off my feet, for all you cared. While you were fawning over that clown, we could have had a busload of foreigners. I could have worked my fingers to the bone. "

"Rubbish! I can hear the bar door open and close even when I'm upstairs. I knew it was dead down here. Cuthbert, over there, was the only new customer to arrive while I was away." She hesitated and grinned to herself, her mind obviously on other things. "Anyway, I wouldn't have missed that experience for the world."

Oswald rose to the bait, swallowing it like a starving trout devouring a juicy mayfly. "I don't want to know the details of what you and that stupid clown got up to, upstairs!"

"Now, now! Jealousy is an awful thing in a grown man. Would I misbehave?"

Oswald narrowed his eyes to mean slits, and set

his mouth in a thin hard line.

Lydia relented and laughed. "I was only kidding. Come over here where we can't be overheard. I'll tell you all that happened."

Reluctantly, Oswald let himself be led into the corner to hear the awful truth.

"I showed Mr Piper to his room, then I told him how to turn on the shower and set it on warm. It can be a bit tricky to work." Her expression changed to wide-eyed amazement. She lowered her voice to a conspiratorial whispered.
"When I made to leave, I was surprised to see he was already under the shower soaping himself down."

"I suppose you couldn't help but look? You Jezebel! Mind you, you've practically seen him naked already! That skin-tight suit doesn't leave much to the imagination. His crotch bulge is about as subtle as the hose pipe those rock stars used to push down their trouser fronts to attract the groupies... or was it gropies?"

Lydia was stung by the accusation. "Well, if it had been Mavis Peabody naked in the shower, you would have made sure you got an eyeful. Wouldn't you?"

Oswald coloured up guiltily at the thought. He had been to see 'The New Curse of the Mummy' five times when Mavis Peabody first took the job of usherette at the cinema, and he didn't even like horror films. He had eaten a dozen ices at each performance, in spite of his sensitive teeth, just so he could peer down the tray at her frozen selection.

Lydia dismissed Oswald's fears. "I'm not interested in Mr Piper. Anyway, he's queer"

Oswald raised his eyebrows and smirked to himself. It appeared the clown was no threat to his love life.

Lydia continued. " He showers with all his clothes on!"

Oswald drew in a sharp breath, pictured the scene and coughed in amazement. She had to be joking. He recovered his composure and was about to question her further when the door from the private quarters swung open and the clown returned to the bar. Mr Piper looked pristine. His black and white suit shone like a brand new one. His jester's hat was completely free of creases and he had washed off all traces of the cobwebs. Oswald stared in astonishment. Surely, it had to be a brand new outfit?

"You showered and dried already, dear?" Lydia patted her guest on the shoulder and winked at Oswald behind his back

"Yes thanks. You were good about the shower. You really give a marvellous service."

Oswald's eyes narrowed again to jealous slits.

"Hussy!" he muttered angrily under his breath. Without waiting to hear any more of her excuses, he stalked across the bar and returned to his seat beside Theo.

Back at the corner table, Theo prattled on about the wax seal while Oswald watched the couple at the bar, unable to tear his jealous gaze from them. In his eyes, Lydia fawned over her new lodger as if there was no one else in the place. The back legs of the horse, tattooed between her breasts, kept flashing into view, as she laughed animatedly and leaned further over the counter. The High Wizard grew more and more angry and frustrated at her behaviour.

"I'll get a small sample of the beeswax sent away for pollen analysis and carbon dating," Theo was saying. "That will prove its age and authenticity."

Oswald did not hear his companion. He sat and smouldered, finding it impossible to ignore the conversation at the bar. The final straw came when Lydia offered to warm the clown's bed for him, before he turned in for the night.

Oswald decided enough was enough. It was time he exercised his unique skills as the High Wizard. Making a secret pass with his hands beneath the table, he muttered a Latin spell and concentrated on getting his revenge. An evil grin spread over his face as he waited for the magic to take effect.

All this time the clown was standing with his back towards the drinkers. Oswald stared intently at the man's tautly clad bottom, watching for the first signs of overheating, for he had cast a red-hot heating spell. With any luck the clown's backside would soon be like a brace of barbecued chickens.

"He wont need an electric blanket or hot water bottle to warm up his bed when I've finished with him," Oswald muttered smugly.

The bar clock ticked peacefully on. Time passed slowly. Theo and Cuthbert enjoyed their beers, while Lydia prattled on to the pied figure at the bar. Oswald never took his eyes off the clown's back, but nothing untoward seemed to be happening. The Fool did not wriggle or show any outward signs of discomfort. The High Wizard looked despairingly at his target and renewed the heating spell, feverishly repeating the magic signs under the cover of the table and frantically reciting the archaic words over and over again, under his breath.

Finally something did happen, but it was not what Oswald was expecting. Peter Piper turned around and smiled knowingly at the High Wizard, as if he fully understood the situation. Oswald coloured up crimson, painfully aware that somehow the clown could tell what was happening. The two rivals stood looking at each other across the empty bar. Suddenly,

Peter Piper's pupils flashed red! Two needle pulses of intense ruby light sped from his hypnotic eyes towards the corner table.

Oswald watched helplessly as his full pint was bathed in a crimson glow and the beer began to bubble and boil. Steam rose from the pint glass. It splintered with a resounding crack! A pool of scalding hot beer spread out over the table, running towards him from the shattered tankard.

Oswald jumped up quickly to avoid the tide of boiling liquid as it headed for the front of his trousers.

That demonstration of his extraordinary powers over, the clown smiled at his adversary, turned abruptly away and limped towards the street door.

"Not so bloody fast!" Oswald hissed between gritted teeth. "I haven't finished with you yet." He focused his powers on the loose carpet in front of the bar and whispered a magic carpet spell. The hem of the rug rose up just as the clown's foot passed over it. The man tripped on the raised edge, lost his balance and hurtled headlong towards the wall.

Lydia gasped and covered her eyes as her new guest cannoned into the jukebox, his head denting the chrome metal front, dislodging a record and causing music to blare out at top volume.

"Round and round, upside down you're turning me…" On cue, Diana Ross crooned over the hapless clown.

For a split second the room stood still, then everyone rushed to the injured man's aid. Oswald, pale with fear and horrified at what he had done, hurried over to the casualty. He silenced the jukebox with one well aimed kick, as he reached the still body. He prayed fervently to himself that the man was not dead.

Lydia screamed aloud, clasped her hands to her tattoo and collapsed behind the bar.

Theo, for the second time that day, bent over the casualty and felt for a pulse. He need not have bothered.

"Well, that was a fine trip." The clown sat up, joking happily in a deep Irish voice. Shaking his wrist free from Theo's grasp, he smiled and said. "Begorra! I'm fine to be sure."

"Sit still, man," Theo insisted. "You may have broken something. You may well go into delayed shock."

Seeing the worried look on Theo's face, Oswald asked. "Is he alright? What's the problem?"

"I can't find a pulse anywhere! You try."

Before Oswald could move, the clown pushed them both away and shouted. "Nonsense. It takes more than a little knock on the head to keep a good barmaid down." The clown leapt to his feet. This time, he was speaking in the unmistakable voice of Lydia Postlethwaite, the pub's landlady!

Theo and Oswald exchanged worried glances. Why did he keep changing his voice to sound like Michael or Lydia? Was it concussion? Had he damaged his brain with the impact? Did he realise what he was saying, and how his voice kept altering?

"I'll take a walk, begorra! The evening air will clear my head like the breeze blows the morning mists from Galway bay." The clown's voice reverted to Michael's again. Shaking off the first aiders, the tall figure in his pristine black and white outfit, left the Dog in a Doublet and limped up the High Street.

Oswald shook his head in amazement. That fellow was a mystery to be sure. He turned to check that the landlady was feeling better. When he found she was fully recovered and needed no help, he decided to return to his cellar workshop and do some more work on his magic.

"I'll have to go, Theo. I'm working on a fine weather spell to ensure sunshine for the day of the town fete. It takes a few days to bring these things to fruition, you understand. And time is getting short." Turning to the landlady, the Druggist suggested sarcastically. "You'd better get that worn rug sorted out. Next time it might be someone important, like me, that trips and injures themselves."

Chapter Seven

Oswald Gotobed left the Dog in a Doublet, making for the chemist shop to carry on with his weather magic. He was seething at his failure to put a stop to his rival and hopping mad at the way the clown had turned the tables on him. He was also insanely jealous of the attention Lydia was paying her new guest. Oswald plotted his revenge on the man, conveniently forgetting his feelings of horror when the man fell onto the juke box.

"I'll show that pied freak it doesn't do to tangle with the High Wizard of the RUFS," Oswald muttered. "Mind you, he obviously knows a thing or two, the way he spoiled my pint of beer. I don't know why I failed to set his bum on fire with my heating spell. But I did get the mat to trip him up. It looks as if the blighter has made himself spell proof. My magic won't work if he knows it's coming, but I can still get outside things to affect him if he's not aware of my intentions. That must be why he didn't notice the rug trick. I suppose he's quite good at magic, really. I wonder where he trained in hypnosis and the esoteric arts?" He would have continued the monologue all the way to his underground workshop had he not been distracted by a familiar, black and white figure, behaving very strangely on the forecourt of Hinman's garage.

Oswald ducked out of sight into the newsagent's doorway and peered through the side window at the clown. He's a funny blighter, the Wizard thought, as he watched the man trying to lubricate his knees with an oilcan.

The clown applied the nozzle of the oilcan to each of his kneecaps. Stretching out his legs as if he was working the lubricant into them, he did several deep knees bends to flex his joints. Obviously satisfied with the effects of Hinman's multigrade engine oil on his creaking joints, he took off towards the river at a fast sprint. All signs of his limp had vanished.

Oswald was puzzled by these antics. He knew a rub down with White Oils helped rheumaticky joints, and the Runford football team swore by the healing effect of Wintergreen Oil, but those remedies never worked that quickly. Overcome with curiosity at this strange behaviour, Oswald decided he would follow the pied figure at a safe distance.

Purposefully, the clown strode along the

riverbank. He seemed to know where he was going, for he stepped out boldly with no hesitation, on his newly oiled legs. Strangely, he appeared to be arguing with himself as he went along. Occasionally he waved his arms about to emphasise a point. Snatches of conversation carried back to Oswald, on the evening air. Sometimes the man spoke in a deep Irish brogue, at other times in the unmistakable fen accent and light feminine tones of Lydia Postlethwaite.

"He's a bloody good mimic as well as a hypnotist and a magician," the Wizard muttered jealously.

The clown halted on the riverside path behind the Fire Station, looked up at the tall brick tower where the firemen hung up their hoses to drain, and smiled in a self-satisfied kind of way. Apparently he was happy to stay by the river, because he sat down on the grassy bank just above a sewerage outfall, pulled off his hat and lay back as if he was taking a rest. There he remained, absolutely still, his shiny head reflecting the sunlight.

Oswald, intrigued by this, hid himself nearby in some tall grass where he could keep watch. An hour passed slowly by but nothing happened. Eventually, he grew tired of waiting and crept back to the High Street to get on with more important things.

The Wizard let himself into the chemist shop and went down to the cellar, where he spent his evening working on his fine weather spells. It was important the town fete enjoyed good weather. The RUFS had decided to set up a fortune telling booth that year. He knew that the more people who patronised the fete, the more money they would make. Oswald passed the evening perfecting his fine weather skills. The evening sun shone obligingly over the market square and time passed pleasantly for him. He didn't give a thought to the clown until he was ready to clear his workbench and go home for the night.

"When I've done here I'll go home via the riverside pathway and see if the blighter is still there," he promised himself.

Before he made for home, the Wizard checked the area behind Runford fire station. He was surprised to find the pied figure was still stretched out in the grass, just as he had been several hours earlier. This was very suspicious behaviour. None of the locals would have spent so long near that smelly sewer outlet. Oswald decided the clown must suffer from blocked sinuses or he was definitely up to no good. He was intrigued by the man's behaviour and crept unseen to his own hideout in the long grass, determined to keep a close eye on him.

The sky was dark before Oswald detected any sign of movement. It was getting chilly by that time and he had almost made up his mind to give up the vigil, convinced that the stranger was still sleeping off the headache he had suffered from his impact with the jukebox. Suddenly, in the glow from a distant streetlight, Oswald saw the black and white figure rise furtively from the grass and tiptoe towards the fire station. This struck him as very suspicious because it appeared the man had been deliberately waiting for the light to fail.

The clown crept stealthily into the yard behind the fire station, keeping to the shadows and stopping every few steps to glance up at the well-lit windows of the fire station recreation room. He did not go to the door of the main building as a legitimate visitor would, but sidled into the open archway at the base of the drying tower.

Oswald followed the pied figure at a distance. This was easy as the white patches on the man's clothes, showed up well in the dim light. The Wizard waited and listened intently for several minutes at the entrance to the yard before he heard the sounds of someone clambering up the iron ladder, inside the tower. Oswald scratched his head. Why would anyone want to go up there? It didn't lead anywhere. Granted it gave an excellent view over the town, second only to the church tower, but that was in the daylight. At night you would see nothing. What was the clown up to? There would be nothing worth stealing, up the tower. Maybe the impact with the jukebox really had turned Peter Piper's mind?

The clown climbed the ladder to the topmost rung and opened up the wooden trapdoor at the top. He stepped onto the flat roof and looked up into the night sky at the stars twinkling above him. Satisfied with the privacy of his surroundings, he lay down on his back, unzipped his suit and stared up into the Milky Way. He seemed to be waiting for something to happen for he stayed wide awake. There was no sign of him falling asleep. He didn't even blink.

Below the clown, Oswald stood motionless in the base of the tower, peering up into the darkness. At first, nothing happened. Then he became aware of a high pitched sound coming from above him. He cupped his hands to his ears and strained to hear the faint sounds. When he did make out the unusual noise, it reminded him of the oscillating tone he heard from his radio, if he accidentally tuned it off station.

"He must have an extremely small transistor set," the Druggist muttered in the darkness. "I didn't see any pocket where he could have had it hidden. Strange really, I could see everything else he had inside that tight fitting suit! I suppose he'll get better radio reception up there, but it's a mystery to me why he's bothering. If it was wartime, I'd think the blighter was an enemy agent receiving secret coded messages." Oswald shrugged his shoulders then had an amusing thought. "Perhaps he's an undercover VAT man working for the Common Market. I'd better warn Malcolm to check the books tomorrow."

The high pitched modulations went on into the night. Oswald began to get bored. In the dark, his imagination worked overtime. The regular patterns of up-and-down notes began to sound like the music of a distant flute. To lessen his boredom, he amused himself by trying to fit the tunes of several popular songs to the half-heard notes. He stayed at the base of the tower for some time, looking upwards and straining his ears to recognise the elusive melodies. At last he became completely bored with the waiting game, and his mind returned to revenging himself on the clown. He considered the possibilities. It appeared his magic spells wouldn't work directly on the person of the clown but they could be made to work on his surroundings.

"What goes up must come down," the Wizard muttered with a grin. He chanted an obscure Latin verse to himself and pointed his finger at the bottom section of the metal ladder. The rungs promptly vanished into thin air. Oswald turned to go, grinning with satisfaction at his plans for the clown's undoing. He tiptoed away, not wishing to be heard, but he didn't manage many steps in the darkness before something startled him.

Something live ran over Oswald's feet! A high pitched squeak rang in his ears! In the gloom he could feel small, living things scurrying on the ground around his ankles. When he stood and held his breath to listen, he became aware of scratching and squeaking sounds all around him. Searching for some explanation, Oswald kicked out tentatively in the darkness. His boot connected with several small, soft, live bundles! He panicked and ran out of the shadow of the tower. Suddenly, by the light from the fire station windows, he saw the whole yard was a heaving mass of small, writhing creatures with grey fury bodies, long tails and small pointed ears. Instantly he realised what they were.

"Rats!" He shrieked. He threw caution aside and ran to escape. The rodents squealed louder as he ploughed through them. He trod on hundreds of the writhing bodies, lost his balance and skidded, sprawling full length among them.

"Gerroff! Gerroff!" Oswald screamed aloud, as numerous river rats buried their sharp teeth in his ankles and wrists, in their attempts to escape from under his struggling body. He scrambled to his feet and tried to brush off his furry attackers, who were still hanging on to him with their sharp little teeth like wingless vampire bats. He ran in a mad panic towards the High Street and the welcome streetlights.

Oswald's cries for help would normally have alerted the fire crew on standby in the recreation room, but that evening the entertainment committee had hired Mavis Peabody to do a programme of exotic dances. At the very time he was fighting off the hoards of rats, she was performing the dance of the seven veils and had just removed the eighth veil. Nothing, short of the whole town burning down, could have possibly disturbed the duty fire crew.

Oswald did not stop running until he reached his home. He let himself into the front door, slamming it shut behind him as if the hounds of hell were in hot pursuit. When he had regained his breath he dropped to his knees and peered out from the letterbox, terrified lest the small bloodthirsty rodents had managed to follow his trail.

It took him half an hour, several glasses of whiskey, and the application of a full bottle of iodine, before he regained his composure and sat down to consider the night's happenings. His mind was full of unanswered questions. Why had the river rats decided to congregate in the fire station yard? What was that strange musical sound emanating from the top of the tower? Did the music have anything to do with the rats congregating? Why the hell had that clown bothered to climb to the very top of the tower, anyway? Surely, not just to listen to his radio?

Oswald poured another stiff drink, tore off his clothes, and ran himself a hot bath. Rat fleas probably bite as much as their hosts, he thought fearfully. He lay back, soaking in the disinfected water, his chin resting on the bubbles and idly wondered what the clown was doing at that moment.

"Maybe he's still up there. Hopefully he's hanging from the ladder, trying to feel for the missing steps in the dark, suspended with his feet on the last rung and still half way up the tower."

Oswald scrubbed his back with a loofah and sighed contentedly. "No doubt the firemen will rescue him in the morning. Then he'll have some explaining to do. He'll think twice before he tangles with me again." He grinned to himself at these thoughts of revenge and sank further down into the luxurious foam.

Chapter Eight

Oswald would not have felt so smug if he had stayed at the base of the fire station tower instead of rushing home for a bath.

Peter Piper climbed down from the tower several hours after Oswald had gone home. He had no problems with the rats as they had all returned to the river by this time. He clambered down the metal ladder until he came to the last rung. One more step and he should have felt the firm ground beneath his feet. But he didn't! He felt for the next rung with his foot and puzzled over the lack of it.

Peter stared down into the gloom and realised he was still suspended several metres above the ground. Somehow the ladder had lost its last section, leaving him stuck up the tower.

"The ladder has dropped off!" The Irish voice stated the obvious.

"So what?" Lydia's voice answered.

The clown didn't seem too perturbed by the

problem. He answered the two voices in his own voice. "So I'd better lower us down. Just thought you might like to know why I was tying this rope onto the bottom rung."

He pulled a fine length of rope from his codpiece and hooked it to the last metal rung. He tested it for bearing his weight then slid down to the ground as easily as an acrobat climbed down from the high trapeze. Once he was safely on the ground, he shook the rope from below. It unhooked from the ladder and coiled itself back in his pouch. He set out along the riverside path, chatting to himself as he walked.

It was getting late by the time the clown returned to the Dog in a Doublet. Last orders had been called and the real Michael Flannegan was staggering out of the pub doorway.

"Goodnight colleen, goodnight colleen... I'll see you in my dreams..." The well-oiled labourer crooned his sentimental farewell to the landlady.

"Goodnight, Michael. Good riddance!" Lydia closed the door behind him and was just going to throw the bolt and make the pub secure for the night, when the clown walked in. He smiled at her and made eye contact.

"You're just in time, love," she gushed at her returning guest. "Do you want some cocoa before we both go up to bed?"

The Fool ignored both invitations and went up to his room alone.

Once she had turned out the downstairs lights and made the pub secure, Lydia climbed the stairs to the private quarters. As she tiptoed along the landing, past the guest bedroom, she noticed there was a bright light shining under her lodger's door.

"He must like reading in bed," she muttered. "I used to like to read a good romance, but I'm too tired these days." She poured herself a stiff nightcap and removed her makeup.

At four o'clock in the morning, when Lydia paid her customary visit to the bathroom, she was surprised to see the light still shining under Peter's bedroom door. It lit up the landing as bright as day. She tutted to herself, assuming the clown had dozed off and left the lights on.

"Maybe he's up and about like me," she muttered hopefully.

Some minutes later, when she returned from the bathroom, she found the light was still blazing. She leaned close to the door and listened carefully, but she could hear no
sound from her guest. She decided to investigate and tapped lightly on the bedroom door.

"Are you awake Mr Piper?" She pressed her ear against the door but she could hear no reply.

Lydia tried again, this time knocking a bit harder. Still she got no response. The landlady decided her guest must have fallen asleep with the light on and left the electric meter ticking. She turned the doorknob noiselessly, eased the door open, and glided into the room, fully expecting to find him fast asleep in his bed. She stopped in the open doorway and surveyed the scene.

Lydia was shocked. The clown was sitting on a bedroom chair in the centre of the room. Behind him, she could see the bed was unused. He had positioned himself immediately beneath the ceiling light so that it shone down fully onto him. He was still wearing his pied suit but he was bare headed. His peculiar hat lay on the bedside table.

Lydia took in all these details before she moved stealthily into the bedroom.

"Good God! He's as bald as a Coot," she muttered under her breath, eyeing the shining bare head. Raising her voice slightly she spoke to the still figure. "Are you alright Mr Piper? That's not a sunlamp you know. It won't give you a tan on your scalp."

There was no reply.

Her curiosity aroused, the landlady tiptoed over to her lodger and stared closely at his shiny, bald head. His scalp was as smooth as a baby's bottom. She reached out and almost touched the smooth skin but drew back her hand just in time, reminding herself she had no business being in Peter Piper's bedroom anyway.

"What a strange man," she whispered as she crept out of the guest's room. Leaving the light turned on, she tip toed back to her bed, uneasy at what she had just seen.

Peter Piper basked under his bedroom light until the sun rose next morning, then he sat in the bay window, leaning his head on the sill and tilting his bare scalp towards the rays of the dawn. By the time he put his jester's cap back on and left his room to go into town, the morning was well advanced. The bar was open and one or two regulars were having an early drink.

"Rats? You say there were thousand of rats on the riverside path? Are you sure you were sober?"

"I was as sober as I am now. And this is my first pint today."

Lydia put down the glass she was polishing and added her comments to the conversation. "That river is a disgrace. It's like an open sewer. No wonder we've got rats, the council do absolutely nothing about it. Next time the mayor comes in here I'll mention it to him. We can't have rats everywhere. We'll all get the plague or something equally nasty."

The clown came through the door into the bar just as the word 'rats' was mentioned. He stopped in his tracks and turned to face the group of drinkers.

"Rats? What's this about rats?" he asked sharply.

"It's nothing. Don't worry about it, my dear. There are no rats here. It's just that someone saw thousands of them down by the river last night."

Peter Piper smiled disarmingly, walked out of the bar and into the street. He turned over this new information in his mind.

"So! Thousands of rats were gathering by the riverside. That's bad." He tutted aloud, for he did not like the sound of that at all. "Last night on the brick tower was not a success. What I urgently need is somewhere high up and private. And it must be well away from rat infested rivers." He shuddered at the thought of all those rodents.

It was a nice bright day. No one took any notice of the jester in his tight black and white outfit, as he strode along the Fen Road, heading for the open countryside. Peter Piper kept his eyes peeled for the vantage point he needed. He was to be disappointed. Mountains, mounds, even substantial molehills, are not plentiful in the Lincolnshire fens. He walked and searched in vain.

By late morning the clown had covered several

miles. He walked deep into the fen farming country. He found himself surrounded by open fields, dotted with the occasional red brick, grey slated farmhouse. He strode along at a steady pace, constantly searching the flat silt fields for somewhere high to stop and rest. In desperation he gave up any hope of finding a natural hill and made for a water tower set in the middle of a grass field next to a farmhouse. The concrete structure rose high above the surrounding flat land. As far as he could see there was no river nearby. There would be no water rats. It would have to do.

Peter demonstrated his acrobatic ability once again, by climbing up the vertical concrete leg of the water tower as easily as a spider crawled up a wall. At the top he lay on his back at the centre of the domed lid of the container, well out of sight of anyone passing by, and set up his radio.

The modulating sound of radio waves spread out from the tower over the peaceful fields like weird flute music, just as it had from the Fire Station tower the night before. As no human was close enough to hear the sounds, the clown felt confident of an uninterrupted afternoon.

Unfortunately, the hearing of rodents is much more acute than that of humans. The high frequency sounds radiating from the tower had an unexpected effect on the resident farm rats. Every rat for miles around was mesmerised by the tones. They stopped their foraging and ran towards the water tower. The word passed among them. The trickles of furry grey bodies banded together into streams. These in turn, became torrents, as the animals tried to find the source of the fascinating music. The faint rustle of tiny paws rose through a gentle throb to a definite drumming on the dirt footpaths, which ran beside the deep-water drains of the fen fields. News spread from rat to rat. Like excited football fans converging on a cup final at Wembly Stadium, they came from far and wide to the South Lincolnshire fens.

Unaware of all this activity, the clown tried desperately to use his radio transmitter. But he received no reply. He feared the worst. They had given him up for lost as they had not heard from him for so long. But still he tried. He couldn't give up because that was his sole purpose for being there. Only when he was disturbed by the noise of a tractor coming through the gate of a nearby field, did he realise he might be spotted loitering on the top of the water tower and that might raise some awkward questions. Peter stopped his transmitting, curled his aerial back into his codpiece and slid down one of the concrete legs, happy to slink off undetected across the pasture to the main road.

Chapter Nine

"I'll take the lot Mr Gotobed. It's the only way I can see of getting rid of them damn rats from my farm." Fred Ransom wrote out a cheque and loaded the entire stock of rat poison onto the back of his pickup truck.

"That's the fifth customer this morning." Malcolm explained to Oswald. "I've already telephoned the wholesalers for more stock of rat poison, but they've run out. It seems we have an epidemic of farm rats in South Lincolnshire."

Oswald, who was busy in the dispensary preparing a love potion for one of his private clients, coughed nervously at the mention of rats. Unconsciously he scratched his wrist where the recent bites had faded to faint red marks. He recalled with a shudder, his own tussle with the thousands of rats in the fire station yard. I wonder if there's a connection, he thought grimly? What if rats from all over the fens had been attracted to Runford for some unknown reason? Maybe his experience was only the tip of the iceberg - the visible one tenth? What if the other nine tenths were out there on the local farms, roaming the fields and causing havoc with the stored crops? The telephone rang, thankfully interrupting his overactive imagination. Oswald answered it.

"Runford Pharmacy. How can we help you...No I'm afraid we've sold out of rat poison...Not in the next week or so. The wholesalers have been cleaned out of all their stock."

Malcolm stood in the dispensary doorway, listening to his brother's conversation. He shook his head in frustration. There was no way the shop could satisfy this overwhelming demand. They had already sold six months stock of rat poison in that one morning.

"Well, leave it with me Mr Giles.Yes I know I produced good weather for your harvest but that's a bit different from killing off billions of rats...Oh! You'd pay that much to be rid of them.... Leave it with me, I'll see what I can come up with." Oswald put down the receiver, the gleam of greed in his eyes.

"What have you in mind, Oswald? You know we haven't the ingredients to make our own brand of rat poison in bulk." Malcolm grunted.

The druggist shrugged his shoulders and went below to his private laboratory. Malcolm stood and thoughtfully watched his back until he was out of sight. He could sense his brother was up to something. From past experience he knew that always spelled trouble.

Below stairs in his workshop, Oswald thumbed through all the magic books in his private collection. He didn't know exactly what he was looking for, but he felt there must be some spell he could adapt, among the hundreds in his notebooks.

"How to attract rats... No! Wrong way round; I want to be rid of them. Perhaps I could reverse the spell and drive them away." He muttered quietly to himself, as he flicked through each leather bound volume.

"How to turn rats into coachmen and footmen...Strewth! I bet that's the old pumpkin into stagecoach recipe. If I change them all into flunkies, the job centre wouldn't cope with the rush. Anyway they'd revert back at midnight!" He dismissed that ancient spell and carried on searching.

"How to turn rats into mice...That won't get rid of the problem. Only reduce it in size. And they probably breed faster!" He continued scanning the pages.

"How to make animals grow bigger...perish the thought!" He shivered at the image of millions of rats as big as dogs, running amok all over the countryside.

"Oswald. There's a Mr Giles come to see you." Malcolm shouted down the cellar stairs.

"Damn the man! I need more time on this one."

Up in the shop Will Giles was impatiently pacing up and down in his muddy green wellies, leaving a trail of fresh mud and pig muck along the tiled floor. His border collie followed closely at his heels, mirroring every impatient step.

"Well, Mr Oswald? Any progress on the rat front?" The farmer asked as soon as the Wizard's head appeared above the counter top.

"I'm still working on it," Oswald said lamely.

"You can forget those bags of spuds I owe you. Another week with these rats and the potato store will be empty. Those damn rodents will have chewed their way through my entire crop!" Will turned angrily away from the counter and stomped out of the shop.

Malcolm, who had watched this exchange with growing concern, tutted loudly to himself.

Oswald turned angrily on his twin, venting his frustration at feeling so useless. "What's the hell's the matter with you, brother? You sound like a broody old hen!"

"I do wish you wouldn't dabble in the occult and promise people you'll work some sort of miracle for them. When you fail, as you are sure to do, it always seems to reflect on our business. You could ruin us!"

Oswald had no answer. He knew his brother was right for once, but he wasn't going to give him the satisfaction of actually admitting it. He stomped angrily down the stairs, to his laboratory and slammed the cellar door loudly shut behind him.

"What I need is inspiration, not brotherly criticism," the Wizard muttered glumly. "Maybe I'll consult the tarot cards, or the runes, or the numerology tables, or the astrology charts, or my crystal ball...or the bloody lot!"

An hour later, having tried every prediction technique he knew, Oswald was still sitting hunched over his workbench, staring at the copious notes he had made during his divination attempts.

"What all this advice boils down to, is this...Large problems require large solutions...That's bloody useful advice, I must say!" He grunted in disgust as he threw the pack of tarot cards back into the desk drawer. "I could have found that much inspiration in a cheap Christmas cracker! I ask you. Isn't it obvious? Of course large problems need big answers. It stands to common sense." Suddenly he hesitated, his frown dissolved and a ghost of a smile flitted over his face. His fertile mind had come up with a reputation saving formula. Without stopping to explain, he rushed up the cellar steps and out of the shop.

"I must slip out, brother. I'll be back for the evening dispensing duty."

"But where are you going? What if someone phones for you?"

"I'll be over at the RUFS library for half an hour, then I'm going out to the fen to see Will Giles."

Malcolm stood glumly behind the chemist counter and watched the retreating figure of his brother. The chemist was used to his brother slipping off whenever the fancy took him, but he was getting fed up with being left to do all the work. With some misgivings he realised that Oswald was whistling cheerfully to himself as he crossed the High street. Malcolm knew that sound only too well. His brother was up to something and that always meant trouble!

Chapter Ten

Oswald soon found what he was looking for among the RUFS comprehensive collection of esoteric books. He copied out the spell, rushed back to the pharmacy and made up the potion immediately. The practical work done, he left the shop in the same mad rush.

"See you later, Malcolm." He shouted to his brother as he hurried through the doorway. He left, only to return a few seconds later, grab a tin of cat food from the pet shelves and run out again.

"Why don't you eat properly?" Malcolm called after him. "At least buy some chips to go with that cat meat." The chemist was rarely sarcastic but his patience was beginning to wear thin at Oswald's wild escapades.

Oswald pushed the packages into his jacket pocket, strapped on his crash helmet and roared out of the back yard, on his old motorbike. A plume of blue smoke followed the classic Triumph Twin as he burned rubber and roared along the fen road towards Will Giles' farm.

When Oswald arrived, the farmyard was alive with hundreds of rats roaming everywhere. They kept popping in and out of the garage and hen houses, scrambling through the hay and racing across the yard. Everywhere Oswald turned was alive with squeaking rodents. Will Giles sure has a big problem, he thought grimly. As soon as he drove across the farmyard and cut his engine, the barn door swung open and the farmer walked out to greet him.

"So, you think you can help? Thank goodness for that. My dogs and the cats are exhausted trying to kill so many rats. My son has spent so long firing his airgun at them he has a blister on his trigger finger, and has run out of ammuntion. Bring your motorbike into the barn. The beggars will eat anything. I'm sure those rubber tyres won't last long out in the yard." Will beckoned the motorcyclist into the shelter of the farm building and quickly closed the doors behind them.

Oswald prised off his crash helmet and looked around him. There were two collie dogs in one corner, sleeping exhausted on a heap of sacks, their tongues lolling out, their breath rasping. Three farm cats stared down at him from the hayloft, their wild green eyes half closed with exhaustion. Will's son waved a bandaged finger at him and grinned sheepishly, as proud of his injury as he would have been of a war wound.

"It looks as if I have arrived just in time. I want to try an experiment. Will, can I borrow your farm cats?"

"You'll get no more help from them. They've had enough. All three have been bitten several times. Blackie has lost half an ear."

"Trust me I'm a wizard with these things. I have prepared a potion to sort the problem out." He sounded confident but it was all bluff.

"Well alright, if you say so, Mr Gotobed. But you'll have a job getting hold of the cats. They're almost wild. They never come into the house and they won't usually let me near them. In fact my daughter Vicki is the only the only person they'll go to."

"Ah! Young Vicki has a way with them, has she? Good. I could do with some help."

"You're out of luck. She's at school until four, then she stays on this evening to attend Tina Stothard's Brownie group."

Oswald frowned. There were always problems. Whatever he tried to do, met with snags. If he couldn't feed the cats personally, he would have to leave the magic potion where the cats could find it, and hope they ate the right amount. It was a good thing he had thought to bring a tin of cat food from the shop.

"Can you get me a tin opener and an old saucer, lad?" he asked the farmer's son.

Oswald tipped the cat meat onto the saucer, poured on his magic powder and stirred the mixture thoroughly with an old fork.

"Here, Kitty, Kitty." He held the meat at arm's length, to show the cats the treat in store for them. Wafting the saucer about in his hand, he let them get the scent, before he placed it in the middle of the barn floor.

Ten minutes later the three men left the barn, closing the door behind them, trapping the three cats inside.

"Leave the dogs out here," Oswald suggested. "They can keep the rats at bay. I don't want any of those bloody rats getting at that doctored food!"

Oswald watched through a knothole in the barn door. He was delighted when all three cats jumped down from the hayloft and sniffed hesitantly at the tinned meat. Blackie, a very pregnant female and the largest of the three, was the first to taste the offering, the other two stood back waiting their turns.

"It's working!" Oswald whispered to Bill and his son. "One of them is eating the food and the others will soon.

Thank goodness they like the flavour. According

to the TV adverts, seven out of ten cats prefer this brand. But, knowing my luck, these moggies might have been the odd three that didn't. Now, we'd better leave them to it."

"Come into the kitchen. Me missus has just taken a meat and potato pie out of the oven. I take it you'll join us for a bite to eat."

Oswald rubbed his hands together in eager anticipation. Will's wife was a good cook and he hadn't taken time out for any lunch. They trooped into the large farm kitchen. The delicious smell of home cooking mingled with the aroma of coffee, Oswald's favourite perfumes, pervaded the air. They tucked into the meal and temporarily forgot the problem of the rats.

Twenty minutes later, with the meat pie just a memory and a dirty dish, they returned to the yard and cautiously swung open the barn door to retrieve the empty saucer.

"Can't see any change in those two. What's this special potion supposed to do? Will it make 'em full of energy?" Will pointed to the two tabby cats who were licking the empty saucer and still crying hungrily. Blackie shot out of the barn and raced across the yard to the shelter of the woodpile.

"She's full of go," Oswald observed.

"Aye, she will be. She's always been top cat in

the yard; especially since she's pregnant. Her appetite has grown as her litter gets nearer being born. She's eating for three at least. I bet she ate the bloody lot. The other two wouldn't get a look in."

Oswald swallowed hard and shook his head from side to side, denying the truth of Will's remark. He had mixed enough magic potion into the meat for all three cats. If Blackie had scoffed the lot there would be trouble.

He gulped nervously and glanced over at the woodpile. In the next few hours that black cat would feel the full effects of a triple dose of growth spell. He shrugged his shoulders and hurried over to his motorbike. It was high time he beat a retreat. It was useless crying over spilled cat meat.

"I must be off now." Oswald pulled on his crash helmet and fired up his motorbike. Shouting above the roar of the twin exhausts, he mouthed. "Let me know how you get on. I expect you'll start to see some results by tonight." But he was careful not to specify exactly what results they could expect. He accelerated out of the yard, relieved to leave this new problem behind him. Hundreds of rats scattered away from the front wheel of his machine as he roared out of the gateway.

All the way back to town, the Wizard tried to estimate the effects of his mistake. He had put down enough doctored food to increase each cat to twice its normal size. That had been his solution to the rat problem: double sized cats would catch many more rats. If Blackie had devoured the entire tin of meat she alone would feel the full effects of the potion. That meant she would grow to twice her size, times a factor of three! That was six times her present size!

"Blackie was about eighteen inches long, if I'm any judge of measurement. That means she'll grow to about...NINE FEET!" The Wizard balked at the thought and swerved dangerously across the road as he momentarily lost his concentration. "That moggie will be as big as a bloody Tiger!"

Oswald pulled over to the grass verge and stopped, cursing himself for using a simple spell that depended on the quantity of potion consumed.

"Now I'll have to reverse the effect. That means getting close enough to administer the antidote. That will not be easy. A nine feet long, wild, black feline could be difficult to approach!"

He kick-started the Triumph motorbike and headed back to Runford, grumbling all the way home at his bad luck. "I bet that damn clown had a hand in this. There was no plague of rats until he decided to listen to his radio at the top of the fire station tower."

Oswald wasn't sure how Peter Piper could be to blame, but he felt in his bones, the stranger must have something to do with the disaster. It could have been second sight that led him to this conclusion. Then again, he was determined to lay the blame on someone other than himself, and the newcomer seemed the best candidate.

"That blighter has been fancying Lydia ever since he arrived here! How am I supposed to make it up with her if there's a rival in the frame? That fact alone is enough to prove he's guilty."

Chapter Eleven

Two days after Oswald's ill fated experiment with Will Giles' farm cats, the first reports of local sightings of the Lincolnshire Black Panther began to circulate in Runford.

A near neighbour of Will's had been awakened in the small hours of the morning by a disturbance in his stock yard. His prize bull had broken through the stout fencing and vanished into the night. Whatever frightened the animal also woke the farmer as it prowled over his rooftop dislodging dozens of slates. It had growled ferociously at him when he leaned out of his bedroom window and shone a torch beam onto it.

"Tell me again." Lydia asked the farmer as she leaned on the bar, her ample bust reflected in the polished mahogany.

"Whatever it was, it had green eyes that shone in the dark. I'd swear it was a giant cat but I was so shocked I dropped the torch into the yard before I managed to get a good look at it. The animal bounded off the roof in one great leap and ran across my fields."

"Is it one of them panthers, like they have on Dartmoor? I've seen 'em mentioned on the posters advertising the Natural History Society lecture. Do you think it has escaped from a zoo or maybe a circus?"

"I rang the police and they say there are no reports of missing big cats. But I know what I saw and it weren't no farm pussy cat!"

Oswald, who was sitting at the corner table having his lunch, listened in shocked silence to this conversation. He had a very good idea of what Will's neighbour had seen, but he wasn't going to mention Blackie or the doctored cat food.

Being market day, several more farmers drifted into the Dog in a Doublet for lunch. They crowded into the bar, tainting the air with the scent of crew yards and muck spreaders. Lydia kept spraying the room with lavender air freshener but it made little difference. Talk was mainly about low market prices and the terrible increase in livestock feed costs but one newcomer stopped the conversation dead.

"Any of you seen this Black Panther?"

Lydia spoke up. "Bill here was telling me about it only ten minutes ago. He reckons it ran up his roof and frightened his prize bull."

"Funny place to tether a bull!"

"Don't be daft, man. The bull was in the stockyard. It broke the fence down and ran off. It took me and the wife half the night to round him up. I'm only pleased he weren't harmed,"

"Then he's bloody lucky. I've two dead sheep with their throats torn out. About half of each carcass was eaten. I ain't seen this killer yet, but when I do it'll get peppered with shot. Me old dad says we need to set some traps, but I'm afraid of harming the dogs or more of me sheep."

"What about stray dogs? Sometimes they worry sheep, don't they?" Oswald piped up from the corner, trying to suggest an alternative and divert their attention away from the truth.

"I suppose a very large dog could have done it, but that panther thing has been sighted over at Will's place and I'm only five miles further down the fen drove. Besides, there would be claw marks if it were dogs. This was a clean bite through the neck."

The Dog in a Doublet bar resounded with suggestions of how to catch the creature before it did any more harm. As the beer consumption increased, the ideas grew more fanciful. Steel gin traps were the most popular suggestion, followed closely by deep pits, covered over with branches and baited with a live sheep, as used by big game hunters in the jungle.

Oswald hoped that Will Giles would not put two and two together and realise that this new menace was his own black cat, in an oversized skin. It was imperative he thought of a way to give that cat the magic antidote before more damage was done. With his mind full of this burning problem he returned to the pharmacy to cover the lunch hour, to allow Malcolm time to go home for his mid-day meal.

At half past one the shop was empty. With all the prescriptions dispensed, Oswald stood at the dispensary bench, considering whether to open another tin of cat food and lace it with a diminishing potion. The shop bell stopped his roving thoughts and alerted him to another customer. An attractive young lady came into the store.

"Hello Tina. Nice to see you again." Oswald eyed Tina Stothard up and down from the privacy of the dispensary, letting his eyes linger on her slim figure, from the metal tips of her high heeled shoes to the top of her neatly combed, blonde hair. "I won't be one minute. I'm just completing a prescription."

"Is Mr Malcolm in?" She queried.

"No. He's at lunch. Will I do?"

"It's about some Natural History Society business. I know your brother is a keen bird watcher. I wondered if he'd seen or heard anything about this

Black Panther that people have reported seeing in the fen? Have any of your other customers mentioned it?"

"Ah! The notorious Lincolnshire panther. I've heard quite a lot about it" The druggist made the most of this opportunity to cash in on his insider knowledge and impress the girl. "I know exactly where it's been sighted and I've a good idea where to look for it."

Tina's eyes widened in surprise. "I didn't know you were a naturalist as well. That's marvellous. Is there any chance you could tell me where it is?"

"I'll do better than that, Tina, I'll show you. When Malcolm gets back from his lunch you can drive us over to the fen and we'll search for it" Oswald was killing two birds with one stone. He wanted an opportunity to get to know the lovely Tina. He also needed to find Blackie, and two pairs of eyes were more likely to locate the cat. Anyway, she was an experienced wild life observer and would have binoculars.

"I'm afraid my cars in dock, Mr Gotobed."

"I haven't one either, but I have a spare crash helmet. You're welcome to ride pillion on my motorbike."

"That's kind of you. I'll slip home, pick up my binoculars, and put on some sensible clothes. I'll change into my trousers and boots. I won't be long."

"Must you?" Oswald mouthed the comment silently, to himself. He would have preferred his passenger to keep on her short leather skirt and high-heeled shoes. The thought of braking hard and feeling those nylon clad legs pressing against him was already exciting him. Tina, oblivious to Oswald's amorous interest, dashed home to get changed .

Chapter Twelve

As soon as Malcolm returned from his lunch break, Oswald made his excuses.

"I have an appointment with a farmer about rat control. I'll try and be back in time for the late surgery." He left the shop before Malcolm could raise any objections.

Oswald drove his motorbike to Cuthbert Stothard's house where he had arranged to pick up Tina. Earlier in the day, he had made a batch of the shrinking potion, which would return the cat to its normal size. He stirred the correct dose of the potion into a tin of cat meat and put it in his saddlebag, hoping he would get near enough to the Black Panther to administer it. The remainder of the potion he hid in his downstairs workshop. The Wizard was pleased to find Tina waiting for him, dressed in her jeans, leather jacket and long boots. He handed her the spare crash helmet.

Oswald drove out to the fen at break neck speed

with Tina seated on the pillion. He knew the girl was not used to motorcycling and hoped she would be frightened enough to hold on to him for dear life. Predictably, she pressed herself tightly against his back and wrapped her arms around his waist. Oswald could feel her grip tighten at every bump and bend in the road. He deliberately rode the bike flat out with the twist grip at full throttle. He made sure they went over every bump and depression, and he took a racing line around each corner.

They parked the motorbike on the drove, just past Will Giles farm, where they could get a good view over vast acres of fen grassland. There was a knot of trees in the corner of one field, but little other cover, for most of the broad fields were separated only by water filled drains. All the hedgerows and trees had been grubbed out to increase farming efficiency. There was no hiding place for a large beast on these open pastures. Tina had suggested the panther would prefer to hide under the cover of trees during the daylight hours.

"If it's out there, we'll see it from here," she assured him. She leaned on a nearby five- barred gate and focused her binoculars on the distant horizon.

Oswald stood well back, admiring the contours of her stretched jeans, pulled tightly over her neat rear end, as she leaned forward. There was something he found very arousing about a pretty young girl bent over a five-barred gate.

"Try scanning that copse over there. Those pigs in the next field seem restless. They're crowded at the far end of the field and I just heard the flurry of pheasants, flying up from the trees," Oswald suggested.

She trained her glasses on the distant knot of trees and peered into the shadows. "You could be right. I think I can just make out a large black dog, or something very similar, lying under one of those bushes."

Oswald was not feeling at all brave but he knew he must find the beast's lair if he was ever going to reverse his terrible mistake.

"I suggest we sneak along that ditch, out of sight of the trees, and try and creep closer to it. We shall soon see if it's the big cat."

He broke a stout stick from a roadside hedge to use as a walking stick.

"Gosh! You're brave Mr Gotobed. But I'm game if you are."

Oswald drew in his breath, held in his paunch and swelled out his chest. Game for what? He thought hopefully. Together they negotiated the drain, edging nearer to the copse, making as little noise as possible. They walked at the base of the bank, near the water's edge, keeping their heads below the top and out of sight. Some fifty yards from their quarry, Tina signalled for them to stop, scrambled up the bank, dropped onto her stomach and popped her head just above the rim of the drain. Like a sniper on reconnaissance, she focused her binoculars on the nearby woods.

"You're right, Mr Gotobed!" she whispered excitedly. "I can see a long black shape basking in the sun. It's partly hidden by a bush, but there's one dark pointed ear clearly visible against the sky. Whatever it is, it's far too big to be a dog."

"Do call me Oswald," the druggist whispered in her ear. He wanted to get away from the formal mode of address and become more familiar with the girl. If he couldn't attract Lydia back to him he saw no reason to become a recluse.

"If we are to work together to capture this panther, we can't bother with ceremony, can we, Tina." He borrowed her binoculars and looked for himself. "Yes. That has got to be our big cat." Handing the binoculars back to the girl and added dramatically. "If you stay here, I'll creep nearer and try to corner it."

"That sound far too dangerous!" Tina shook her head in disbelief, but admiration shone out of her blue eyes.

Patting his jacket pocket to assure himself he still had the doped cat food in his inside pocket, Oswald crawled off towards the woodland.

Ten minutes later the Wizard was within a few yards of the huge black cat and could see it easily. He hesitated on his stomach, watching the animal lazily flicking its tail as it basked in the warmth of the afternoon sun. He could clearly see the green glint in its eyes, which were almost closed, and the pink of its mouth, which was lolling open.

Good grief! What enormous pointed teeth! Discretion told him to venture no nearer. He felt in his pocket and painstakingly eased out the tin of cat food.

The cat still lay on its back, licking its distended stomach, engrossed in its grooming and oblivious to the stalker. Oswald eased back the tin lid and shook the contents onto the bare patch of earth, immediately in front of his face.

"Come on Blackie." He spoke quietly. "Come on puss, puss. Nice tin of cat food for you."

The cat pricked up its good ear and turned its baleful green eyes towards the intruder.

Oswald paused with the tin of meat poised in the air, a reassuring smile on his face. The cat rose lazily to its feet and padded towards him. The druggist stood his ground, held his breath and silently prayed.

Blackie stopped a few feet away from the prone

figure. She could smell the delicious meat but under that large exterior, she was still a wary farm cat

"Come on, Blackie. Nice meat. Nice Pussy."

Suddenly, the peace of the afternoon was shattered! A figure shot up from the side of the drain. Tina, waving her binoculars in one hand and Oswald's walking stick in the other, shouted loudly and ran across the field towards them. The cat took one startled look at this intruder before it turned and fled like the wind. Oswald's mouth dropped open in disbelief. He rolled over onto his back and cursed under his breath. If he'd had just two more minutes with the cat, he might have succeeded. What the hell did the girl think she was doing? To his amazement and delight, Tina ran straight to him and wrapped her arms around him. She lifted his head from the ground and pulled his face hard against her breast.

"Are you alright, Oswald? Did it bite you?"

"No. No. I'm fine. What ever came over you? Another minute and it would have come to me. I might have captured it."

"Oh dear! I'm sorry! I was so nervous for you, I dropped my binoculars. When I picked them up and managed to focus on you again, I could see you were lying on the ground and the panther was standing over you. I panicked. It could have been attacking you. I thought you might be injured!"

Philosophically, Oswald dismissed his disappointment and revelled in the unexpected attention, snuggling closer to her slim young body, listening to the thump of her racing heart through her leather jacket. In the circumstances he felt it was almost worth losing the opportunity to deal with the cat.

They lay like that until the girl's panic subsided. She shook her head in disbelief. "I've never seen anything so brave, Oswald. From over there, you looked as if you were actually talking to the animal."

"I was talking to it. It's only like an overgrown domestic cat, isn't it? I'm sure an experienced big game hunter would have done the same thing. Although, I suppose I did throw caution to the winCome to think of it, at this precise moment, I can't think of many people who might be that brave."

"You're far too modest." She gave him a kiss on his forehead and rose to her feet. She didn't notice him as he closed his eyes and smiled blissfully up at her. "It will be miles away by now. What a pity! Still, I did see it, and I can add this sighting to my county mammal records, along with your notes on how it looked at close quarters."

Oswald waited for Tina to move back towards the drain before he attempted to scoop the doped cat food back into the tin. Unfortunately it had been scattered when Blackie ran away, and it proved impossible to recover. He gathered a handful of dry leaves and soil to cover the food over, just in case any other creature fancied the meat. If he didn't hide it, strange foxes or rats were always a possibility! He pushed the empty container into his jacket pocket.

All the way back to Runford, Oswald was preoccupied with planning his next move. When he had time to reflect on his failure, it was little consolation to him that Tina thought he was a hero and wrapped herself even closer to him on each bend in the road. He knew he couldn't leave matters as they were. Two sheep were already dead, farmers and livestock were frightened out of their wits, and the potential for even worse disasters was getting greater by the day. He knew he must return on his own to the copse and hope the cat used that area regularly. Maybe it was making a den there to have its litter, he thought hopefully. It was certainly no use bringing Tina back with him. Much as he would enjoy her company on a night watch, he couldn't risk her realising he was responsible for the problem in the first place. Anyway, he found her presence too much of a distraction. He'd have to try to think of some other excuse to enjoy her company another time, in more relaxed circumstances.

Chapter Thirteen

The pharmacy was getting busy when Oswald returned from his wasted attempt to dose the panther. His brother was relieved to see him as the afternoon surgery had just started and prescriptions were piling up in the waiting tray on the dispensary bench.

"About time. I thought you were never coming back." Malcolm sounded irritable and tired from being left to do all the work alone.

"Well, I'm here now. Let's drop the subject and get on with it." Oswald's mind was still full of his other problems but he put those aside and started printing labels and counting tablets.

The brothers worked well together and soon reduced the numbers that were waiting. After an hour the afternoon surgery tailed off and prescriptions came into the pharmacy only in dribs and drabs. Malcolm had just made them both a cup of tea when the local doctor called in to see them.

"Keeping you busy, doc?" Oswald nodded

knowingly at the heap of completed prescriptions in the out tray.

"Aye. It's been an unusual surgery today."

Oswald raised an eyebrow and enquired. "Have we an epidemic of something on our hands?" Then realising the doctor was the only one of them not drinking tea, he asked. "Have you time for a cuppa?"

The doctor looked at his watch and nodded. "Why not. I wanted a professional word with you both anyway." He pulled up a stool and sat down with a sigh.

Oswald brought the doctor's tea. The three of them drank in silence.

Finally, Malcolm put down his empty cup and asked. "What can we do for you. then? You know we'll help if we can."

"Have you a copy of the latest county medical bulletin. I've lost mine somewhere in the filing system at the surgery."

Oswald took down a box file from the top shelf and passed it to the doctor. The brothers waited while he put on his glasses and flicked back and forth through the index.

"No. Nothing there." The doctor closed the file.

"Problems, doc?"

"Not really. I have had three patients complaining of the same unusual condition. I wondered if there were any more reported cases. I can't think we have an epidemic in the county."

Malcolm frowned. "Epidemic? What's the problem?"

"I won't be breaking any confidentiality if I tell you two we have a rash of sleepwalkers on our hands."

"Sleepwalkers!" Oswald almost laughed aloud. "That's nothing new, surely?"

"Well when three people come to see me, all describing exactly the same unusual circumstances and non of them has ever sleepwalked before to their knowledge, I have to take notice."

Malcolm said nothing, but he did look decidedly sheepish and drummed his fingers on the bench. The doctor didn't notice his nervousness, but Oswald did.

Oswald was curious. "Tell me, doc, what are these strange circumstances?"

"Each one of the patients has had the same vivid dream. They tell me they can hear pan pipes or a flute paying outside their window. Each one got out of bed and tried to open the window to follow the music. One female patient actually opened the window and started to climb out. Thank goodness she woke up in time, as she sleeps above her place of business!"

"Could be very tricky, sleepwalking all over the place."

Malcolm looked askance at his brother. "Why should it be tricky?"

"Well, think about it, Malcolm. What if it was the vicar and he slept in the nude. Or what of it was your wife and she had nothing on. As I said, it could be tricky. If the newspapers or the police found out about it, we'd have the place alive with tabloid journalists." Turning to the doctor, Oswald asked. "You don't think it could be an ear problem? Maybe the sound they hear is like a ringing in the head?"

"No. I considered that first, but my tests show there's no ear or sinus problems."

"How can you hope to treat it then?"

"That's the problem. Sleeping tablets wouldn't make much difference, unless I used such a high dose, I rendered them paralytic, so they couldn't walk. I hate to think what they'd be like next morning. I can't use drugs to keep them awake. That's not possible on a long term basis."

"What have you done with them so far?"

"I've asked them each to keep a diary and come to see me next month. I might refer them to the county psychiatry service if the situation doesn't improve."

At the mention of the psychiatrist, Malcolm choked violently and dashed to the sink to get a glass of water.

The doctor rose from his stool. "Must go. Duty

calls...You should make yourself a good cough bottle for that throat, Malcolm." He nodded goodbye to Oswald and left the shop.

Oswald leaned back on the dispensary bench, shook his head sadly, and eyed his brother thoughtfully.

"Well? What?" Malcolm put down his glass and glared at his brother.

"Well what about your sleepwalking then?"

"What do you mean?"

"Come off it brother. I'm your twin. I know you better than you know yourself. I saw your reaction to the doc's news."

Malcolm looked away sheepishly.

"You have been having these nightmares, haven't you."

"Well...yes! As a matter of fact it happened last night."

"I was going to suggest to the doc that maybe his patients were people with problems on their minds - folk who had guilty consciences. But now you've joined them, I can't see it. You are a perfect example of a God fearing Christian, with a conscience as clear as bottled drinking water. Unless you're keeping some dastardly guilty secret from me?" Oswald grinned at the thought and gently poked fun at his brother. "Does Freda know you've got another woman? Have you told her you're a drug smuggler? Is it the vicar you fancy?"

Malcolm looked upset and shook his head emphatically.

"Don't be facetious. It's no laughing matter. I wake up in the morning, feeling as if I've never been to sleep."

Oswald dropped the humour. "It's really getting to you, isn't it. I am genuinely sorry. I suppose if either of us is to have conscience troubles, it ought to be me."

Malcolm grasped at the last remark. "You're not having them, are you?"

"Having what? Nightmares, that cause sleepwalking? No way! I have a couple of whiskeys before I go to bed and I sleep like a baby until the morning. Judging by the tidy state of my bedclothes I hardly move at all. I suppose I'm paralytic!"

Malcolm rinsed the teacups and his glass under the hot tap and went back to the shop counter without another word, making it obvious that the subject of his sleepwalking was closed.

Oswald turned the doctor's conversation over in his mind. He wondered who the other sleepwalkers were. As Runford was a small town, it must be someone he knew. I wouldn't mind bumping into Tina Stothard, Mavis Peabody or even Lydia

Postlethwaite in the buff, one of these dark nights, he thought hopefully, but knowing my luck it will be Malcolm or the vicar.

With the afternoon rush over and the close of business not far off, Oswald's thoughts returned to Blackie, the Black Panther, and how he was going to get close enough to dose it with the shrinking potion. His lack of progress was worrying. If anyone was due for nightmares, he must be a prime candidate.

Chapter Fourteen

It was dark by the time Oswald returned alone to the copse on Will Giles' land, where he and Tina had disturbed the Black Panther. Unfortunately, there was no sign of Blackie in the area. By the light of his torch, he could see that the drugged meat was still where he had left it. If only the damn cat had eaten the bait, his worries would be over. The Wizard lay beneath the trees in the moonlight, passing his time visualising Tina sleepwalking in the nude, while he waited for some sign of the farm cat.

It was not silent amongst the trees. In the dark, strange sounds came from all around him. He heard the distant bleats and grunts of sheep and pigs settling down for the night. An owl hooted as it flew over the copse. There were a few high pitched squeaks he couldn't identify, but guessed they might come from the rats. He strained his eyes, but could see none of the rodents. Perhaps they were staying underground to avoid Blackie? If that was the case he was pleased that his plan had at least half worked.

At midnight a church clock struck twelve. The sound of the distant bell carried across the fields on the damp night air. As the last strike died away, there was a faint rustling from the nearby drain. Oswald held his breath and strained his senses to listen. There it was again, hardly audible. Suddenly he detected a large dark shadow slinking silently over the grass towards him. He saw the black shape in the moonlight as it left the concealment of the ditch. It was Blackie, she was as big as ever! He took out another tin of meat and stirred in a dose of reducing potion. By the time the cat had entered the woods he was prepared to feed the mixture to her.

Lying on his back, holding his breath, Oswald silently recited a vanishing spell. He was thankful that casting invisibility spells was one of the accomplishments he had already perfected as High Wizard. Slowly his outline grew fuzzy as he vanished into thin air. The big cat, obviously a creature of habit, returned to the very same spot it had occupied before. It lay full length under the bushes, where it could keep a watchful eye on the surrounding fields. Oswald noted it did not seem to be at ease. He realised that it could probably sense his presence. Maybe it was picking up his scent. Perhaps I shouldn't have splashed on that cheap after-shave this morning, he thought. After a while, the animal cradled its head on its front paws and relaxed, the green eyes reduced to thin slits as it catnapped in the moonlight.

Oswald wriggled forward on his stomach, the tin of cat food held up in one hand. To a casual observer it would have looked like a flying tin of meat, moving along jerkily, about twelve inches above the ground. The cat raised its head and turned to look in the Wizard's direction. Oswald froze into immobility, then slowly lowered the opened tin to the ground. Gradually, inch by inch, he withdrew his hand.

Blackie drew back her lips in a snarl, showing her sharp white fangs. A faint warning hiss carried on the night air. The Wizard was petrified. He knew the cat couldn't actually see him but he realised that cats had very keen senses. Some people spoke of them having a sixth sense. Perhaps it was aware of his presence? Then, the awful truth struck him. He had forgotten to put the fluence on his shoes and socks. They would still be visible! In desperation he started to whisper."Come on Blackie. Nice pussy. Here's a nice, tasty tin of meat for you."

The cat narrowed its eyes and shrunk back on its hind legs, coiling like a powerful steel spring. Suddenly, it sprang forward and dived on the tin. In the confusion Oswald rolled away from the action, his shoes still visible, flaying the air. Blackie sniffed at the tin then backed away, panting and mewing. She seemed very preoccupied with washing her stomach and rolling on her back. She had completely lost interest in the tin of cat meat or Oswald's feet.

It slowly dawned on Oswald, the animal could be about to give birth to her litter. No wonder she'd lost interest in eating. He shrugged his shoulders and breathed a deep sigh of resignation. Without thinking, he spoke aloud to himself. "Why couldn't the damn cat have eaten the tin of meat first?"

Blackie reared into the air at this voice from nowhere. She pawed the ground, a cat searching for a mouse in the pitch darkness. When she sprang, her gleaming claws dug deep into the bare soil just in front of Oswald's nose. The Wizard rolled under the nearest bush, closed his eyes and started to pray. He knew most of him was invisible but he was still afraid those terrible claws might find him by accident.

Slowly the cat overcame her fright and started to sniff the night air, drawing the unfamiliar odour of the Wizard's after-shave over her twitching nose and sensing his presence. Gradually Blackie crept towards the invisible figure, lying prone among the bushes. Oswald held his breath and closed his eyes. The cat bent down and sniffed warily at his feet then moved up his body to his face. Her whiskers tickled his nose as she moved her head from side to side, trying to make sense of what she had found. With the animal's long hairs brushing against his nostrils, the Wizard's need to sneeze became unstoppable.

"Aaaa....tishoo! Atishooooo!"

The sneezing took Blackie completely by surprise. The cat rose into the air as if she'd been shot from a cannon. From his position on the ground, Oswald could see under all four of the animal's huge padded feet. As soon as its feet hit the earth the cat raced off into the darkness leaving Oswald shaking but relieved.

Once he had regained his composure Oswald realised he had seen the last of the cat for that night. He picked his way across the fields to his motorbike, and headed for home, taking his time and wallowing in his feelings of failure. He knew he should have succeeded in dosing the cat that time. He had come as close to his quarry as he wanted to, but when it came to the critical stage of the operation, he had failed again. If he could only judge things right, the cat would be back to its normal size by morning. If only he hadn't worn that damn after-shave! If only he had remembered to vanish his shoes and socks! If only...if only...

Reversing the invisibility spell, in case some unfortunate traveller noticed his riderless motorbike speeding along the open road, he headed for Runford.

The last thing he wanted was stories of a phantom motorcyclist, to add to the Black Panther scare. The more he thought about it, the more his feelings of failure grew. Somewhere in the Lincolnshire fens there would soon be a family of Black Panthers! He took a full bottle of whiskey to bed with him to drown his disappointment.

Chapter Fifteen

The first Lydia knew of Peter Piper's tendency to wander aimlessly about the pub premises was when he walked into her bathroom as she was enjoying her morning soak.

Earlier that morning she had set her hair and shaved her legs. She stood in front of the long mirror and parted her silk dressing gown to admire her full figure from the side view.

"Not bad for my age." She pulled in her tummy and stuck out her ample chest. "Why I'm still single I shall never know. Although this work of art can be an embarrassment." She turned her body to view it full frontal and frowned as her eyes took in the tattoo of a hunting scene she had commissioned in her wilder, younger days. The huntsmen rode down between the twin mounds of her breasts. The hounds spilled over her nicely rounded stomach, skirting her navel. The fox they were pursuing had almost gone to ground, his brush curled up from her pubic hair, the rest of him had already vanished between her thighs.

"Anyway, some men have found it erotic. Even Oswald said he liked chasing Reynard." She shrugged her shoulders, knowing that she was stuck with the tattoo, like it or not.

She threw off her gown and stepped into her bath. Luckily, she was up to her chin in pink bubbles when her lodger stumbled uninvited into her bathroom.

"Eh up, love! This is my private bathroom. Guests have to use the one off the landing." She submerged herself further in the deep foam, pressing her back against the bottom of the bath, trying to hide her body. She glanced quickly down at herself, embarrassed in case the galloping Master of the Hunt or the foxhounds rounding her dimpled navel, were visible through the hot bath water. Lydia was certain the fox vanishing into its earth between her thighs was well submerged and definitely not on view. The lady need not have worried. The frothy bubbles formed an impenetrable layer of fine foam above her naked figure. Anyway, Peter Piper seemed not one bit interested in her charms, naked or otherwise.

"I am just checking for optimum reception," he muttered vaguely.

"Get out before I give you a hot reception!" Lydia shouted, throwing her loofah at him as she submerged herself even deeper in the suds.

The clown stood in the centre of the small bathroom with his head inclined at an angle, like some keen ornithologist, listening for the first cuckoo of spring, then he wandered out through the open door as if no one was there but himself.

"Shut that bloody door behind you!" Lydia screamed.

He hesitated in the doorway then absentmindedly pulled the bathroom door shut behind him. She leapt out of the bath, dashed dripping across the fake fur rug and pushed the bolt across the door. She was fuming. Not only had he interrupted her in her bath, but he'd totally ignored her as well!

"Checking for reception? He wasn't even carrying a portable TV or radio. Perhaps it was just an excuse to see me in the buff." She coloured up at the thought, especially as he'd not paid any attention to her. Perhaps she'd lost her charms? What if he didn't fancy her? Lydia stared at herself in the steamed up mirror and absentmindedly tidied the curl of stray hair peeping from beneath her pink plastic bath cap.

Peter Piper marched along the corridor. His head was still inclined at the same attentive angle. He had sent his messages out and was banking on a reply coming through, but he had a problem. The buildings tended to screen off the radio waves and he was afraid he might miss the answering signal while he was indoors. In his quest for better reception he tried the kitchen and the private sitting room but neither of these satisfied him. Finally he went into the public bar and lingered in various parts of the room to test the reception there.

When Lydia came down into the bar to prepare for opening time, her lodger was sat at a corner table near the open window, a far away look on his face, like a patient in a crowded doctor's waiting room, cut off from his surroundings and awaiting his call. He appeared to be rather switched off, for he was considering his problems and oblivious to what was going on around him.

Lydia put aside her feelings of frustration.

"You feeling alright, love?" She asked him. She felt concerned for him. Judging by his appearance and his complete lack of interest in her, he couldn't be feeling normal.

The clown took several seconds to realise he was being spoken to. He waved one hand vaguely in the air.

"Ah yes.the reception in here is fine thank you." He turned away from her and sank back into his reverie.

Lydia didn't like this show of complete

disinterest. She was not used to men seeing her in the bath, then ignoring her. It had never happened before.

"I don't mind you using the bar as a sitting room when we are closed," she told him, "but once we open you'd better order a drink or you'll set the regulars a bad example. I can't have everyone thinking this is a free waiting room. If you want to stay here you'll have to buy a drink, Do you understand me, dearie?"

Peter Piper just smiled and nodded absentmindedly.

At opening time, the regulars filled the bar. Michael Flannegan, who had just been paid, emptied his pay packet on the counter and ordered drinks all round.

"What about your lodger?" Michael pointed to the black and white figure sitting rigidly at the far table.

"What do you fancy to drink?" Lydia shouted.

Peter did not reply.

"Go over and wake him up, Michael," she suggested, as she pulled a pint of Guinness for the Irishman.

"What would you be thinking of drinking with me?"

"Oh! Sorry. A pint of distilled water or some light engine oil please."

Michael scratched his head and looked

enquiringly at the landlady.

"He'll have fruit juice and like it," she exclaimed impatiently! She liked a man with a sense of humour but there was a time and place for everything.

"I don't know what I was thinking of, expecting him to fancy me. Never mix business with pleasure," she grumbled under her breath.

Michael placed the glass of orange in front of the solitary figure and retreated to the bar. Peter didn't make any move to taste the offering or even to acknowledge the gift.

"Has he been drinking heavily already?"

"Not here he's not," Lydia replied huffily.

Mavis Peabody, the local good time girl, called in for a bottle of single malt whiskey. She liked to entertain her well-off gentlemen customers in the manner they were used to at home. Gone were the days when a post action cigarette filled the bill. Nowadays, people smoked less. Nowadays she felt obliged to supply drinks and light refreshments to help them recover. It was always added to the bill as a further service charge.

"I'll have a mineral water, please." Mavis pouted at Lydia. She knew she was not really welcome in the Dog in a Doublet. Lydia made her hostility very clear whenever the girl ventured into the bar.

"I'll take it over there." Mavis pointed to the table furthest from the bar, where the clown was sitting alone, minding his own business.

"Can I sit here next to you, dear?" she asked after she'd made herself comfortable. Peter stirred into consciousness and smiled absentmindedly at her.

"Anything new in trousers and she's there." Lydia hissed out the corner of her mouth. "I bet she knows more about the men in this neck of the fens than the Social Security, the Child Support Agency and the Inland Revenue combined."

Peter, fully alert now that he was not alone, heard the whispers. His super sensitive hearing missed nothing. He took Lydia's comments at face value and decided that Mavis would be a useful contact for him. If she knew so much about everyone, perhaps this young female could have information of value to him? He smiled animatedly and flashed his green eyes at her.

"You're new, darling. I haven't seen you here before." Mavis gushed at her companion. "If you're staying in town a day or two perhaps I could show you some of the more interesting sights." She eased the front of her blouse open and hoisted her short skirt a little higher on her thighs. There weren't many interesting sights not already on view.

The Clown glowed at her benignly. The green

eyes glanced up and down her well-rounded figure, taking in the details of her leather skirt and her transparent blouse with a rather nice cameo at the neck. Suddenly his eyes took on a fixed, hypnotic stare. His gaze bore deeply into the girl's brain. Mavis never was one to struggle, it wasn't in her nature. She succumbed immediately, falling willingly under his hypnotic spell

The clown read her mind as easily as flicking through a book, but he failed to understand most of the contents. He was not well versed in the kinky sexual habits of Mavis's customers. He may not have understood the finer points of the Karma Sutra or the Perfumed Garden but he did understand that knowledge was power and the sexual foibles of the more prominent members of her clientele could prove extremely useful to him. The secret habits of George Willis, the Chief Constable of the county, particularly interested him.

The two figures sat across the bar table, staring into each other's eyes and smiling blithely. Several of the customers noticed the situation, nudged each other's elbows and nodded knowingly at each other.

"Could be love." Michael volunteered.

"I bet it's lust." Lydia scowled and slammed the till drawer shut with unaccustomed vigour, mixing all the change. "I'd better warn him. She's not the kind of girl I would want my lodgers associating with." She sniffed at the thought of Peter preferring that little tart fully clothed to her in the bath, and stared hard at the back of the clown's neck, willing him to break off the encounter.

He was aware of the landlady's wishes but he ignored her. What he had learned about the Chief Constable would be put to excellent use when the opportunity arose. He plotted how he could make use of the knowledge and smiled even wider at the prospects.

Chapter Sixteen

On her way home from the Dog in a Doublet, Mavis Peabody called in at Theo Willis's antique shop on the pretext of looking at a framed picture displayed in the window. Theo was out. As usual, Dora, his wife was minding the shop.

"Can I take a look at that rather nice watercolour in the window?"

Dora Willis sniffed to herself as if her customer was wearing pink paraffin instead of a subtle touch of Channel down her cleavage.

"It's an exquisite watercolour by Peter De Wint. You won't be able to afford it."

"It's my birthday soon. I have a gentleman friend who might like to buy it for me."

I bet you have. Dora thought cattily, her mouth drawn into a tight line of censure. He'll buy it for you for services rendered above the chip shop, no doubt. And the nearest you'll get to a birthday is your birthday suit! Then her eyes narrowed as she noticed the beautiful antique cameo Mavis was wearing. She recognised it instantly. Theo had bought it privately and was supposed to have sent it away for a minor repair to the safety chain. Seething inside she took the watercolour out of the window, steeled herself to switch on a convincing smile and handed the framed picture to Mavis.

"Nice antique cameo, dear. You have good taste," Dora observed, trying to sound nonchalant.

"Oh! Do you think so?" Mavis pressed her blouse flat around the brooch with her manicured fingers, stretching the silky material taught over her bare breast, then stopped to admire herself in a Regency wall mirror, turning first right and then left to see herself in the best light. "It was a gift from a gentleman friend."

Dora Willis set her teeth into a fixed grin. With a supreme effort she stayed looking cool, although she was boiling inside. If Theo could afford to pay this little tart for her sexual services, giving away their valuable stock to secure her favours, it was time he upped her housekeeping and treated her to a holiday somewhere exotic. She watched Mavis slink out of the shop and across the street before she replaced the watercolour in pride of place in the window. She would keep a wary eye on that valuable picture, just in case Theo suggested sending it away for restoration and cleaning.

Dora stood in the window and looked down the street. In the distance she noticed Theo walking towards home. When he met up with Mavis, he stopped for a chat. Their heads moved close together. The girl seemed to giggle coyly. Theo glanced furtively around them to check no one was watching their tete a tete. Dora stepped back from the plate glass window and nodded gravely to herself. It looked very much as if Mavis Peabody would soon be earning a Peter de Wint painting for her services.

"Over my dead body!" Dora vowed aloud.

Five minutes after Mavis had left the shop Theo returned, flushed and excited from the RUFS library and his meeting with the girl.

"You look very pleased with yourself," Dora grunted. "What have you done? Exchanged a two pence piece for a rare coin on the vicar's collection plate, again?"

Theo ignored the scathing reference to one of his earlier business successes and pulled the wax seal from his jacket pocket.

"This is a unique medieval seal." He waved the beeswax disc under his wife's nose in triumph, anxious to justify his extra good humour. "I've been researching its origins and I have come up with an amazing discovery."

She nodded with feigned interest, but her

thoughts were on her errant husband and on that little tart, Mavis Peabody.

"It's not just an early seal with the prior's badge on it. Oh no! It is a magic restraining spell."

Dora opened her eyes wide in pretend amazement, before lowering her head and narrowing them to calculating slits. That's not all you've been researching. You dirty old sod! she thought angrily.

"It's rather like a chastity belt. It will keep any contents safe. It can be strung across a doorway and the occupant cannot get out. If I secured it around a box, the lid would never open. It's a sort of magic medieval security system."

Flora looked at the dusty wax seal and was unimpressed. She doubted these marvellous properties but she nodded in agreement with her husband, just to humour him. Visions of sewing it onto the front of Mavis Peabody's knickers, floated into her mind, but she dismissed the idea. I don't suppose she wears them, she thought cattily.

Theo unlocked the wall safe in the office and placed the seal inside. With his back still towards his wife he said. "I might be out late after tea this evening, dear. Got to help Oswald Gotobed look up some things at the library."

Dora was beside herself with anger, she knew he daren't lie to her like that if he was facing her and she could see his expression. She said nothing, but thought a great deal. Looking up something in the library, my foot! You're going to look up some skirt above the chip shop! If you've arranged to see Oswald Gotobed, I've arranged an appointment with the Pope to discuss contraception.

After tea Theo grew visibly restless. He checked his watch every few minutes and pretended to watch the news, but the shifty look on his face gave him away. Dora noticed the tell tale signs and was not at all surprised when he announced he intended to shower and change before he went across to the RUFS building. He was taking an awful lot of trouble with his appearance just to see Oswald Gotobed and do some research!

"She's just a gal who can't say no..." Theo's baritone voice echoed from the bedroom as he spruced himself up for his alleged stint at the library. Dora sat in the lounge and fumed. She knew her husband did not fancy her. They had not enjoyed a physical relationship for years. But she resented him looking elsewhere, especially as he paid for his pleasure with the business stock, and used her as free labour to mind the shop, look after the house and fill all his other needs. After all, he was the one who had insisted on separate rooms in the first place. As he sang happily, preening himself for his date, her resentment erupted. Dora looked around for some way to thwart his intentions. It was bad enough Theo wanting another woman, but paying her with their valuable antiques was the last straw. She toyed with the idea of hitting him over the head with a Georgian brass candlestick, but she knew she would finish up in gaol. Suddenly the wax seal came into her mind. What if it did work? What if it really was a restraining spell? There were more subtle ways of using it than as a chastity belt for Miss Peabody.

Dora worked fast. While she could still hear her husband singing in his room, she retrieved the disc from the wall safe.

It took only a minute to thread one of Theo's pyjama cords through the holes in the wax and string it across his bedroom door. She used drawing pins to secure it each side. It was the desperate act of a scorned woman, but she had nothing to lose. She sat down in front of the television to watch her programmes, keeping one ear cocked for her husband's departure.

After the late news Dora switched off the TV and tiptoed to Theo's bedroom door. She knelt down and listened attentively at the keyhole. There was no sound coming from the room. She could have been forgiven for thinking her husband had actually gone out, if she hadn't been on guard in the lounge all evening. Slowly she turned the doorknob and edged open the door a sliver, so that she could peep into his bedroom. There on the bed, lay her husband. He was fast asleep, still dressed in his outdoor clothes. The air wafting through the narrow aperture, smelled strongly of his favourite after-shave and cologne but he was flat out on the bed, snoring gently. Dora chuckled silently to herself, eased the door shut and quietly removed the pyjama chord. If the magic had really worked and he hadn't fallen asleep purely by coincidence, she would keep this success to herself and use the wax seal in the future to keep wandering lover boy safely at home.

Chapter Seventeen

Saturday dawned with bright sunshine, which augured well for the success of the Runford town fete. Good weather always ensured the punters came out in their hundreds.

Oswald put this fortunate state of affairs down to his knowledge of weather magic and the spell he had cast for the occasion. Doubters would have said it was just coincidence. Whatever the reason, it promised to be a busy day at the annual fete.

Oswald Gotobed and his brother were both heavily involved in the event that year and employed a locum chemist for the day so that both could have the day off and take part. Malcolm would conduct the church choir and planned to lead a concert of light music from the bandstand in the centre of the park. Oswald had set up a booth for a member of the RUFS fortune telling group to·read the tarot cards and try their hands at crystal gazing. The High Wizard did not intend to get involved in the work himself, feeling it was way below his rank and importance to stoop to that sort of end-of-pier charade, and he had no intention of being tied as he enjoyed seeing what the fair had to offer.

"I know you're not a real Romany. Everybody local knows your dad was a rat catcher and not a gypsy, but for goodness sake try and enter into the spirit of the thing!" He chided the unlucky volunteer. "Do try and look a bit more like a real gypsy. A coloured headscarf tied around your head would be better than a tea towel with 'A present from Skegness' printed across it!"

"It's alright for you. You haven't got to sit here all morning and make a fool of yourself." Oswald ignored the complaint.

Malcolm rehearsed the choir while the church organist tried to tune up the portable harmonium, pedalling furiously to keep up the air pressure. His legs were a blur as he fought bravely against failing air pressure because the hungry vestry mice had gnawed giant holes in the thin leather bellows.

George Willis, the Chief Constable of the county, and his brother Theo, walked through the early morning bustle, smiling benignly on all and sundry, trying to rally the workers.

"Looks like we'll have a fine day, George."

"Sure to be. I've ordered it. Lords can do that, you know," George said, only half jokingly. He had recently bought the Lordship of the Manor of Runford at Sotherbys auction of obsolete titles, and was revelling in his new status.

"Well it's all in a good cause," Theo said lamely.

"I hope all will be ready for my opening speech at ten o'clock sharp. This stall doesn't look very good." The Chief Constable grumbled as he stood by and watched old Fred Hinman struggling to erect his Punch and Judy tent.

"I'll just give Fred·a hand," Theo volunteered, glad to escape from his brother's side for five minutes.

Fred Hinman was the local garage owner but being well past retiring age, the serious engineering work was left to his grandsons. Fred was a well loved local character. The old fellow had performed his puppet show for the children as long as anyone cared to remember. He willingly did his turn at local fetes and at children's parties, at their homes or at school.

"I remember you doing the Punch and Judy when I was a boy," Theo told him as he tightened the guy ropes on the red striped booth.

"I've done it every year since the war," Fred said proudly.

His good deed done, Theo hurried to catch up with his brother who was completing his round of inspection with as much thoroughness as he used to check the new recruits on the passing out parade at the police college.

"Smarten yourself up man, you're a disgrace to the force," George ordered the young police officer at the gate. Not because police constable Poole was sloppily dressed, but just to impress on the man his own superior rank. Poole saluted the Chief Constable smartly, clicking his highly polished heels together like a Spanish dancer's castanets.

As the chief constable moved on, a clown in a black and white suit sauntered through the turnstile, waving aside the request to buy a ticket.

"Must be one of the performers," constable Poole muttered, and let him pass.

Theo tugged at his brother's sleeve and whispered in his ear. "See that clown over there. The one who's just come in."

George looked and nodded.

"He's been in town for a day or two. I'm told he may be up to no good. He tried to steal money from the chemist's shop and he head butted the jukebox in the local pub. I'd say he needs watching."

George narrowed his eyes to steely slits, a trick he had learned from watching TV interrogation scenes. He stared after the pied stranger and called back over his shoulder. "Keep an eye on that clown,

Poole. I'll tolerate no sort of criminal activities on my home patch."

Peter Piper hesitated. Even though he seemed to be well out of normal earshot, his acute hearing had picked up the conversation. He turned to look at the trio at the gate, especially the uniformed officer. The clown always recognised authority when he saw it. Recollections of earlier brushes with the law, stirred in his memory. His staring did not go unnoticed.

"He knows we are on to him." George observed out of the corner of his mouth. "He has guilt written all over him."

Fred Hinman prepared for the show to come. He hung his puppets up inside the booth and laid out his props on the shelf below the stage opening. He had not had time to practise his act before the fete, so he decided to check all was in order by having a small rehearsal. The old man moistened his swizzle in a glass of cider and positioned it in the roof of his mouth. Holding a puppet high above his head he parted the velvet curtains.

"That's the way to do it." Mr Punch uttered his time honoured opening line in the high pitched squeaky voice that was his trademark.

"Here I am Mr Punch," Judy trilled as she went up on stage.

"Ain't she a beauty? There's a nose. Give us a

kiss. Let's dance."

The two puppets danced together, swirling above Fred's bald head in a frenzied waltz.

The clown stopped in his tracks when he heard the strange voice produced by the swizzle. He looked about him for the source of this novelty, for he had never heard anything quite like it before.

"Jesus!But that's a strange little clown with a hump back. Could he be a real leprechaun? I like his jester's hat, that I do." Peter muttered, in a perfect imitation of Michael Flannegan's voice.

"Take that! You silly old woman." Mr Punch aimed a savage blow at his wife, knocking her off the stage.

"Hello, hello, hello!" A policeman puppet appeared from below and proceeded to set about Punch with his wooden truncheon, chasing him about the small stage and hitting him mercilessly about the head.

Peter Piper looked on in amazement. His sympathies were all with the clown. He glanced back at the gate where constable Poole was standing, black baton hanging at his side, the sight was not wasted on him. His eyes glowed angrily with realisation.

Chapter Eighteen

The Young Farmer's stand at the Runford fete proved a great success. They always seemed to produce such imaginative attractions. This year it was exceptionally busy even though it was still rather early in the day.

They had persuaded Mavis Peabody to strip down to her lace underwear and sit prettily on a plank of wood suspended above a tank of water. The sign promised, for a mere pound coin the punters could throw five wooden balls at a target placed beside her. If the throwers were accurate and hit the centre of the target, the unfortunate girl would drop into the bath of water. The challenge proved irresistible, especially as her lingerie was white nylon and might well prove to be transparent once it was wetted.

Oswald spent ten pounds on trying to unseat the girl before he worked out that the target was nailed into place. It was only the encouraging smiles he kept getting from Mavis that had kept him trying.

George Willis, still on his round of inspection, stopped at the young farmer's stall and eyed the attraction.

"Must show willing and set a good example." He rolled up his sleeves and smiled at his brother. The Chief Constable hurled the wooden balls with the force of a hand grenade, completely missing the bull's eye. For the first time that day, Mavis leapt off her perch and plunged obligingly into the water. There was a roar of approval from most of the crowd standing by.

"It's a fix." Oswald muttered in disgust. But he waited for the girl to reappear, hoping he could see through her wet underwear.

George hurried forward, gallantly offering her his hand to help her step out of the cold bath. There was no opportunity for the onlookers to ogle as he quickly wrapped a bath towel around her body, playing the attentive gentleman.

"Here, take this note," he hissed in her ear. A screwed up piece of paper passed secretly between them, finding a temporary home in her damp bra. George winked conspiratorially at her and turned back to the crowd.

Peter Piper waited for the Punch and Judy rehearsal to stop, then he ducked under the back awning of the striped tent and fixed his smile on Fred

Hinman.

Five minutes later the clown left the old man sitting dazed in his tent. The pied figure now carried a puppet on each of his outstretched hands. He worked them enthusiastically as he walked along.

"That's the way to do it, begorra!" Irish Punch chortled.

"Sure you would say that, you drunken hunchback," Judy answered, in the unmistakable voice of Lydia, the pub landlady.

A crowd soon gathered to watch the clown, who was waving the two puppets at arms length and arguing loudly with himself, in two well known, local voices. The man continued his act, totally oblivious to the interest he was arousing.

Tina Stothard had brought her Brownie troupe to entertain the public with an exhibition of campfire singing. As a special treat she had promised them they could see the Punch and Judy show first. The girls were very disappointed when Fred Hinman could not perform his show but soon cheered up when they noticed the clown was putting on a puppet show.

The Brownies wormed their way to the front of the crowd surrounding the clown, and sat down to enjoy the entertainment. The pack leader, pleased that her group were off her hands for ten minutes, took the opportunity to go to the refreshment tent and to the ladies loo. She shouted to the eldest Brownie before she departed.

"Vicki, make sure they behave themselves. I'll only be a few minutes." Then she hurried off towards the marquees.

If Tina had only stayed to listen to the clown's performance, she would have been shocked at the language he used, and she would never have left the girls anywhere near him. When she eventually returned to pick up her young charges, she found them engrossed in the spectacle of the clown's puppetry. She didn't know it, but they were especially pleased with his bad language. They proved very reluctant to move.

"Come away girls. We have to rehearse our songs for the performance," Tina ordered her Brownies.

"But Miss. You promised us we could see the Punch and Judy. It isn't fair!"

Tina turned a deaf ear to their pleas and ushered her pack to the rehearsal tent.

"But Miss, you did promise us." Vicki Giles whined at her.

"We'll see if there's time later. If not, I'll have a word with Fred Hinman and book him to entertain us at one of our Brownie meetings." She led the group away to rehearse, still ignorant about why her charges were so interested in the Punch and Judy man.

Malcolm Gotobed was very concerned at the clown's performance.

"Is he alright? Do you think he's been at the drink already?" Malcolm asked the Chief Constable as the clown's arm movements and the stilted dialogue grew ever wilder. Irish oaths and building site swearing liberally littered the conversation. Judy would not be outdone and gave as good as she got. The real Lydia Postlethwaite had an enviable command of colourful phrases, when she was clearing the bar of late night drunks. She was often described as a screaming fishwife on those occasions. Judy was very like her in this respect.

George Willis was horrified at what he was hearing. He could see the children crowding closer to the clown, sniggering loudly, eager to increase their grasp of adult vocabulary. Malcolm Gotobed held his hands up in horror. The vicar covered his ears with both hands and tried to usher the choir off the stage and out of earshot of the spectacle.

"Constable Poole." George shouted for his man. "Get this fool out of here and lock him up. He's causing a breach of the peace."

The pride of the Lincolnshire constabulary charged into action, truncheon raised and handcuffs jangling at the ready.

The clown stopped his monologue and smiled disarmingly at his assailant, meeting the officer's gaze, eye to eye.

Poole stopped in mid pounce. His upraised arm and truncheon dropped to his side. For several seconds the two men at stared at each other. Members of the crowd, watching the drama, held their breath, unsure of what to expect next, but they were hoping for trouble.

"I'll come quietly, officer. It's a fair cop."

To everyone's disappointment, the clown appeared to give in. Waving the Punch and Judy dolls aloft, he repeated his surrender in a loud voice

"It's a fair cop. It is to be sure. You can put that shillelagh away. I'll come quietly."

Constable Poole marched the clown away from the scene, taking the path that passed out of view behind the beer tent, to escape the attention of the gawking crowds.

The Chief Constable, anxious to bask in the glory of this very public arrest, followed some distance behind them. But George Willis was not prepared for what he found when he caught up with his officer behind the beer tent. It was an unwelcome sight. Poole was lying on the grass, apparently unconscious or fast asleep. The clown was creeping stealthily away from the scene, the stolen glove puppets still held high on his hands.

"Hold on there, clown. Where do you think you're going?" George bellowed.

The clown turned around to face him and smiled disarmingly. A pulsating green light shot from his eyes. By the time Theo arrived, panting from the effort of running, the whole incident was over.

"There's been a misunderstanding," the Chief Constable assured his brother. "This fine entertainer was doing nothing wrong. We must have misheard him." He patted the clown on the back, pushed a ten-pound note into his hand and apologised profusely.

Theo stood open mouthed at this unique generosity, but he knew, from bitter experience, it wasn't worth his breath trying to argue with his brother because George was always right.

"Don't just stand there like a Venus Flytrap. We must get to the main stage. I must make my speech and officially open this year's fete." George walked briskly towards the rostrum, talking volubly as he went. "I want to take this opportunity to impress on the townspeople the importance of our environment. We must look after our clean country air. We must protect our children from breathing in exhaust fumes. I am going to persuade them to stop using their cars and to walk or cycle everywhere. It's better for their health and the countryside."

Theo's mouth fell open even wider. His brother was well known for going everywhere in his car. His sister in law had once sarcastically suggested a drive-in loo, on the ground floor of the manor house, just so George could use his wheels when he was taken short.

George mounted the stage, grasped the microphone and began his speech. "Ladies and gentlemen before I declare this fete officially open. I have an important message for you all. I am worried about the environment. I know you all enjoy your trips in the family car at the weekend and to do your shopping. But I want you to give a thought to the damage you are doing to the air and to your children lungs. Think of the little ones…"

The crowd stifled a yawn and shuffled its feet. They were anxious to be enjoying the fete and did not want reminding of their duty, besides, everyone knew George Willis ran the largest car in the town and he used it all the time. His pleas fell on deaf ears. They looked at each other and asked.

"Why doesn't he take his own advice?"

"As an example to you all I am going to stop using my car at every possible opportunity. I will set you all a good example." George put his hand over his heart and struck a sincere pose.

"Is that the prize porker from the Pig Bowling

Alley flying by again?" someone shouted.

George continued with his sermon unabashed before finally declaring the Runford fete properly open.

The fete was a great success. Mavis Peabody obligingly took the plunge every ten pounds or so, but she and the vicar had insisted on certain improvements to the spectacle. She made sure there was warm water and Eau de Cologne bubble bath in the tank and the vicar insisted she exchange her see-through underwear for a respectable, one-piece, bathing suit.

Gypsy Oswald Gotobed did a roaring trade. The Wizard had been forced to stand in for his acolyte when the first four punters had insisted on cash refunds. t had almost come to a fight in the beginning. The original gypsy's predictions had been so ludicrously stupid that no one would swallow them. With the RUFS credibility at stake, to say nothing of their bank balance, Oswald rose manfully to the occasion. Reluctantly he dismissed the gypsy and took on the fortune telling job himself.

With a little elementary crystal gazing, he had predicted the winner of every race at Market Rasen racecourse that afternoon. It was only when an irate local bookmaker begged him to stop and offered a substantial bribe, he relented and stopped giving racing tips.

Malcolm conducted a boisterous rendering of gospel songs and had the crowds singing along and begging for more. On the whole it was a most successful day for both of the Gotobed twins.

Unfortunately the Punch and Judy show had to be cancelled. The main characters had gone missing and the operator was in a complete daze. Some of the children were upset but, on the whole, people were sympathetic and understanding, when Fred Hinman's grandson came to take the old fellow and his booth, home in the garage break down truck.

As Theo was heard to remark, "The poor old fellow wasn't himself. Maybe he's been overdoing things. After all, he has performed the Punch and Judy show at every town fete since the war."

Cuthbert Stothard was in charge of the traditional Bowling for a Pig stall. In the interests of safety, this being the sort of contest brawny farm lads entered, he had placed a high stack of straw bales across the end of the bowling lane. Behind these bales, completely hidden from the prying eyes of the public, Peter Piper lay on his back and spent the afternoon playing with his glove puppets. It was while he was relaxing in the privacy of this open-air venue, he managed to get good radio reception.

"Sure but I t'ink its time for me and you to return

to me home," Punch declared.

"And what's that got to do with me?" Judy replied.

"You're coming with me, me precious colleen. Yourself and the other human specimens I've chosen. Me masters have asked me to take some live human friends with me, as well as the information I've gathered. You're all welcome, except that horrible Chief Constable. Mary Mother of God! I couldn't stand his company for long."

"What will you do about the Chief Constable?"

"He'll get his just desserts tonight. I've already sewn the seeds of his downfall."

At five o'clock, after the fete had closed its gates and the stragglers had gone home, Oswald, Malcolm and Theo helped the scouts and young farmers to clean up the litter. George Willis, true to form, made his excuses and left as the work began.

"Urgent police business to attend to. Must keep the rule of law on track. Got to ring the Lord Lieutenant. Don't forget about my comments on the environment." Turning to constable Poole he had insisted. "You are not to use a police patrol car unless it's a matter of life and death. Do you understand my orders, constable?"

"How am I supposed to get about the area then, sir?"

"We still have the old police bicycles at the back of the station. You're a fit young constable. Use one of them." George had walked to his chauffeur driven car and then surprised them all.

"You can take the car back to the garage. I'm walking home."

It was the first time ever!

Poole sadly shook his head. It looked as if the chief really meant what he had said.

Chapter Twenty

At half past four, Tina Stothard rounded up her Brownie pack. The town fete was fast drawing to a close.

"Follow me, girls. No dawdling. We have a party laid out at the Brownie hut to round off the day and I have a surprise for you all afterwards."

Vicki Giles made sure all the girls lined up in pairs then fell in at the front beside Brown Owl. "What's this surprise, ma'am? Have you made us an iced cake or something?"

Tina smiled knowingly and shook her head. "It's a secret. You'll find out soon enough."

Tina would not divulge the nature of the entertainment she had booked for them. During the afternoon she had tried to contact Fred Hinman, to arrange for him to give the Brownies their own puppet show, but the old chap was nowhere to be found at the fete. Finally, someone told her he had been taken home, as he was not well.

"Oh dear! I wanted him to do his Punch and Judy show for the Brownies. That is a pity. They will be disappointed."

"That's a shame, dear. But I do believe there's a clown here somewhere at the fete, who does the Punch and Judy. I've seen him with the puppets over near the Bowling for a Pig stand. Why don't you ask him?"

Tina jumped at this suggestion. "My dad's running that stall. I'll see if he knows where the clown is." She hurried off to find her father.

Tina did find Peter Piper. Her father told her the man was resting on the straw bales behind the bowling alley and seemed to be listening to his radio. At first the clown wasn't enthusiastic about doing a puppet show for her, but when she explained he would be disappointing over twenty young girls, and he realised they were the Brownies who had been watching him earlier in the day, he relented and agreed to do an act.

"Come to the brownie hut at about half past five. If you knock at the side door, I'll smuggle you secretly onto the stage and we can surprise them," Tina explained, then realising the clown was not a local man, she asked. "You do know where the brownie hut is, I suppose?"

"Indeed, that I do my colleen." The clown worked the

Punch doll and answered in his broad Irish accent.

Tina clapped her hands with delight at his expertise and the accurate imitation of Michael Flannegan's voice.

"My Brownies will love you." She assured him. She was thrilled to think they would get something different from this performer. It was a shame old Fred wasn't well, but they had all seen his act dozens of times before. This new puppeteer, with different characters and voices, would be a refreshing change for them. It had all worked out well in the end.

The Brownies enjoyed the refreshments. The crisps, jellies, faerie cakes and ice cream all vanished quickly and without trace. A day at the fete had sharpened their appetites. The girls were extremely hungry, as most of them had eaten their packed lunches by mid morning. Tina waited until all the plates and dishes were cleared away then she clapped her hands for their attention.

"Quiet please. I have a special surprise for you." The girls stopped chasing each other and listened obediently.

"I know you were disappointed you did not see Mr Hinman's show this morning. That's why I've asked that nice clown to come here this evening and give us his new version of a Punch and Judy show."

The brownies clapped to show their delight.

They had not expected a second chance to hear the clown's unique dialogue.

Tina pulled back the curtains on their small stage to reveal Peter Piper sitting on a kitchen chair, with Punch and Judy sitting on his knees.

"Give him a big hand." She led the applause as she returned to her seat at the back of the hall.

"That's the way to do it." Mr Punch kissed Judy passionately, groped her backside, and launched into his time honoured routine.

"Here I am Mr Punch. You dirty old man!" Judy, alias Lydia Postlethwait, answered.

"Ain't she a beauty. There's a cleavage! Begorra! Give us another kiss. Lets dance."

The two puppets swirled together on the clown's knee, embracing each other in a passionate Tango. The tone was definitely low brow and the content was for adults only.

The brownies were enthralled with the show. They listened intently to the puppets, hanging on every naughty word and every smutty innuendo. They did not seem to mind that there were only two glove puppets, instead of the usual large cast. They even enjoyed Mr Punch's Irish accent and Judy's habit of calling "Time gentlemen please!" at every opportunity.

Tina was at the back of the hall, eating a

sandwich. She could not hear the dialogue too clearly. It was some time before the true nature of the clown's act became apparent to her.

She frowned and cupped her hand to her ear, in an effort to check what was being said, but the loud laughter and squeals of delight from her young charges drowned out most of the words. Finally, worried about certain half-heard phrases, she left her seat and walked to the front of the hall to put her mind at rest.

"Give us a pint of bitter and have one for yourself, Mrs Punch. And I'll have a kiss and a packet of crisps on account, until after closing time," Mr Punch shouted.

Judy set about her husband, hitting him with both fists and swearing at him.

Tina was shocked. The girls rolled about with laughter. Tina stormed onto the stage.

"This is hardly fit for young impressionable girls. I think we've heard enough of..." She got no further.

The clown turned his piercing gaze on her. Green light pulsed out of his eyes, putting her into an instant trance. The brownies thought this was all part of the act, and applauded vigorously. Tina walked stiffly back to her seat and had no more to say.

As a finale the Clown invited the girls to come up onto the stage, to meet Mr Punch. As they filed by, one at once, and shook hands with the puppet, Peter stared into their eyes and put each of them into an instant trance. They queued up to meet the puppet, giggling and pushing each other. One by one each girl returned to her seat as subdued and quiet as Brown Owl. Never had an audience of children been so well behaved.

Slowly each Brownie filed onto the stage, hesitated in front of the clown and was introduced to the puppets. Peter Piper had hypnotised about ten of them in this way, when he was interrupted by some of the parents arriving to take their daughters home. Two of the girls' mothers and one sheepish father stood at the back of the hall, watching the proceeding with interest. The clown decided against carrying on with his act, in case the parents realised what he was really doing. He stood up and held the puppets aloft.

"Sure but it is time I was getting down to the pub." Mr Punch told the audience.

"Then I'd better get there first to open up." Judy took a final bow.

Peter Piper shook the Judy glove off his hand and clicked his fingers at the room. Tina and the girls he had managed to hypnotise, immediately snapped out of their trances. They yawned and stretched as if they had dozed off after their meal. They were all totally unaware of what had happened to them.

Tina mounted the stage and held up her hands for silence. "We must show our appreciation to Mr Piper for standing in for Mr Hinman so professionally." She led the applause.

The Brownies, now their normal noisy selves, rushed to get their coats and ran to the door to be picked up by their parents.

"Mum, you should have seen the Punch and Judy. It was good." Vicki Giles told her mother.

"Yes dear. Now hurry up. I have to get home to prepare your father's tea."

"Mum, Is Blackie back yet?" Vicki asked as they went out to the car. The girl was still upset at the disappearance of her favourite cat.

"No dear. But I wouldn't worry. She's probably found somewhere quiet to have her kittens. She'll bring them back to the farm when their eyes are open. Now, where's Felicity? Her mum and dad asked me to drop her off as we passed their house."

Vicki grabbed Felicity's hand and led her out to the Range Rover. She was almost two years older than her friend, and felt very superior. As children will, she tried to impress her friend by showing how much more grown up she was. "Mum, can I drive us home?"

Her mother laughed out loud. "Your dad might let you take the wheel down in the hay field, but you're certainly not driving the car on the road, young lady."

"Oh mum!" Vicki whined, but it was to no avail.

The clown packed his puppets into a carrier bag and made his way back to the Dog in a Doublet. He hummed an Irish melody as he walked. He was extremely pleased with his day's work.

Chapter Twenty One

The routine at the manor house on a Saturday evening was always the same. George Willis and his lady wife had high tea in the dining room, then moved into the drawing room where they sat each side of the fireplace like a pair of fire dogs. They rarely spoke or even looked at each other. It was that kind of marriage.

That particular evening Muriel Willis was reading her library book while George sat and fidgeted. He kept looking at the clock and getting up to glance through the window at the state of the daylight.

Muriel was interested in her latest sex-and-shopping romance, but not too engrossed in it to prevent her keeping a watchful eye on her husband. She knew only too well that Saturday night was his usual night for extramarital sex. He would soon be making some lame excuse to leave. I don't suppose I should complain, she reflected. After all, he doesn't bother me with his disgusting habits any more. Thank God! He hasn't been near me for twenty years, not since I refused to dress up in a silly uniform for him and satisfy his perversions. Muriel chuckled aloud to herself at the recollection.

"Good book dear?" George raised an enquiring eyebrow.

"Oh yes...excellent. She's a good author." But she was actually laughing at her own memories of the last fling she had with her husband.

He had always insisted she put on a nurse's uniform, handcuffed him to their four poster bed and administered colonic irrigation. Disgusting! She shivered with revulsion at the memory of it. But that time she had satisfied his appetite for the bizarre, once and for all. Instead of warm soapy water in the enema she had substituted a whole bottle of his favourite after-shave. Since that unforgettable night he hadn't bothered to ask her for more.

"I'll go out for my usual Saturday evening ride." George said, in as nonchalant a voice as he could muster. "An hour or two travelling the bye-ways of the county, admiring the moonlight over the fens and listening to the calls of the night birds, will settle my dinner and help me sleep."

"That's alright, dear. I don't need the car."

"I'm not using the car. Oh no! I need to set an example and save the environment. It wouldn't do for the locals to see their Lord of the Manor gallivanting about in his Rolls."

She put down her book, took off her reading glasses and stared at him in amazement. This was totally out of character.

"How pray, do you intend to travel, then?"

"I'll go...on ...on my...er...our old bicycle," he spluttered.

"The tyres will need pumping up. It's ages since it was used." She observed sarcastically, turning back to her book to hide her smile.

George went out to the garage and made a call on his mobile phone.

"Mavis? It's me. You got my note. I will pick you up on the corner as usual Make sure you wear the uniform and be prepared for a quick getaway. You'll recognise me because I'll be wearing my convict's gear."

The Chief Constable's favourite sex game was cops and robbers. He liked to play the criminal and let Mavis Peabody pretend to be the long arm of the law. In her case he thought she was more the long legs of the law.

George rummaged in the back of his garage and brought out his convict's costume. It was a creation of his own design, made from an old pair of his pyjamas. He had painted broad black arrows all over them with indian ink. Immediately he put on the uniform he was a changed man. No longer was he George Willis, Chief Constable and law abiding Lord of the Manor. He became Naughty George the fugitive cat burglar and sex offender. Disguised as his alter ego, he could make mad passionate love to policewoman Mavis Peabody with non of his usual hang ups.

Usually George donned his broad-arrowed pyjama suit, and completely covered it with a long dark overcoat. He liked to drive into town disguised in a black mask with a trilby hat pulled well down over his face, pretending he was a character from an American gangster movie. He always picked up Mavis outside the chip shop, stopping only momentarily to let her jump into the car beside him. He always kept the car engine revving. It was a risky business for a highly respected police officer to pick up a prostitute like that, but the very thrill of kerb crawling and flouting the normal decent rules of human behaviour added spice to his love life.

That Saturday evening there was a problem. For no particular reason he could remember, he had chosen to deny himself the use of his car. Poor George had no way of knowing that the pied clown had planted a strong hypnotic suggestion in his subconscious, just so that the local law would be hampered by a lack of fast reliable transport.

In the corner of the Manor House garage stood the old tandem, that Muriel and George had used to tour South Devon on their honeymoon. He pulled it from under the rolls of worn carpet and wheeled the old machine out. He pumped up the bicycle tyres, liberally oiled the bearings with three-in-one oil and dusted off the saddles. Everything seemed fine. He hummed contentedly at his success. But there were unforeseen problems. When he climbed astride the bicycle and started to pedal, his overcoat proved too long. The hem caught in the front wheel and almost toppled him off again!

"Damn it! I'll have to go without the coat. Lucky it's a dark evening so no one will notice me."

George Willis cycled down his pebbled driveway and out onto the main road. His wife heard his crunching departure and stood at the drawing room window, peeping out over the front garden. The velvet curtains shook visibly. The sight of a pantomime convict, complete with black facemask and gangster trilby hat, wobbling unsteadily down the drive on an old tandem, was all too much for Muriel. She collapsed helplessly onto the window seat, tears of laughter running down her face.

Just outside the town, the solitary cyclist passed

by an empty telephone booth. He glanced towards it apprehensively, but the area looked deserted. Everything appeared to be going to plan, but he didn't see the trouble that was lurking in the shadows.

The clown ducked down as his victim pedalled by.

"He's taken to heart our instructions to save the environment." Michael's voice spoke quietly from behind the telephone box.

"We'd better make that phone call, now." Judy suggested.

The clown rang the police station, disguised his voice and asked for constable Poole.

"Evening, Poole." The commanding tones of the Chief Constable boomed down the phone line.

"Evening, sir."

"I've just had an urgent tip off. There is a notorious sex maniac making for Runford town centre. We think he will try and pick up a prostitute outside the chip shop. Make sure you arrest the blackguard. You'll have no difficulty recognising him. He's an escaped prisoner. He's still wearing his convict's uniform but he's disguised his face with a black mask. Make a good job of this one Poole and promotion might well be in the offing."

"But I've only got my bike, sir. No cars to be used. Your orders, if you remember."

"Don't panic man. He's on a tandem. You'll have no difficulty spotting him and you'd better not fail me. Don't forget, this could be your chance of making sergeant, Poole. I'll expect a full report on my desk in the morning."

Constable Poole put down the phone and swore to himself. All the same, with the promise of promotion ringing in his ears, he chose the best bicycle from the station yard and hastily pumped up the tyres.

Chapter Twenty Two

Mavis Peabody prepared herself for her evening's assignment. She knew exactly what pleased the Lord of the Manor and it was worth the effort. She was always well paid for their little charades and he was far from demanding as a lover.

She showered, shaved her legs, set her hair and manicured her nails. Then she put on the policewoman's uniform that George had obtained secretly from county police stores, just so she could play her part in his fantasies.

"Funny how some men can't resist women in uniform." She spoke to her own reflection in the mirror above the bed. "I can't see it myself. I don't think I could fancy a romp with the lollypop man. He'd still be a drippy nosed pensioner, even in his best uniform."

She donned the blue jacket and white blouse; easing the shortened miniskirt up over her hips and tugging the hem down to cover the tops of her black stockings. The regulation hat with its chequered band and a pair of black leather ankle boots completed the ensemble. She didn't bother with underwear. Standing in front of the long mirror at the foot of the bed, she appraised her reflection. The prostitute smiled approvingly at the saucy policewoman she saw smiling back at her.

Downstairs, the chip shop was busy. Dozens of teenage lads were buying their suppers before they went out on the beer. They considered it dangerous to be sick on an empty stomach.

Saturday night was always busy like that. The crowded pavement could have made things difficult for her, but Mavis never had to wait long before the black Rolls purred to a halt at the kerbside and she leapt into the passenger seat beside her lover. Normally she had no trouble, as it all happened so smoothly. The girl looked forward to her car ride for she enjoyed the feel of the luxury upholstery against her bare thighs and buttocks, as her short skirt rode up. The sensual touch of that cold leather always turned her on and the sight of her legs did wonders for her escort.

Mavis checked her wristwatch and went briskly down the stairs and out onto the pavement. She knew this part of the charade helped to give her lover a thrill. The very act of picking up his illicit date in a public place, helped George to perform.

She stood on the edge of the pavement, in the pool of light from the chip shop window, and hoisted her skirt up slightly to show a sliver of white thigh.

"You busy, love? Fancy one of each and a local sausage?" A hopeful teenage lad asked her.

"Push off, kid." She spat the words at him, but she kept a fixed smiled on her face, in case anyone was looking. Under her breath she whispered. "Come on George. Don't keep me waiting out here forever. I'm too conspicuous, dressed like this."

Oswald Gotobed had had a tiring day at the fete. He decided to treat himself to a hot supper. He picked up his fish and chips. This time they were wrapped in the Economist as all the copies of the Financial Times had been used earlier. He noticed Mavis Peabody and lingered outside the fish shop before he crossed the High Street to the chemist shop, where he had intended to try out some more of his weather magic.

Smiling hopefully, Oswald passed the time of day with the girl. She pointedly ignored him. He left her alone, guessing she was waiting for someone in particular.

After another long five minutes of peering along the darkened street and suffering the lewd suggestions of every spotty teenage lad who fancied a hot supper, Mavis was getting very agitated.

"Two more minutes and that's your lot, Chief Constable Willis," she muttered angrily.

She checked her watch for the hundredth time, and cursed under her breath. She tugged her skirt hem down and pulled in her chest, trying to look less inviting. Just as she felt she could wait no longer, and was about to give up her vigil, a tandem drew up at the kerbside.

"Pst! Pst! Jump on my back seat."

"Push off you pervert before I...!" Mavis exclaimed angrily, then she recognised the convict costume.

Police Constable Poole had made his bicycle ready and stationed himself in the entrance to the Hole-in-the-Wall passage. He was hidden in deep shadow but he could see all that went on in the marketplace and beyond. He noted Mavis Peabody in her police uniform in front of the chip shop, but he kept hidden and awaited developments.

"I could have her for impersonating a police officer," he murmured softly. "But then she could claim it was only for a fancy dress party." Poole watched the teenage lads making their improper suggestions to the girl and was surprised that she didn't seem to take notice of any of them. Even more surprising, she ignored Oswald Gotobed's advances. Everybody knew he was loaded with money and could well afford her prices.

"She's definitely waiting for a special client. The Chief was right." He rubbed his hands together at the thoughts of his promised promotion. Sergeant Poole was a title that had the ring of authority about it. And the pay and conditions were much better. He'd tell his wife she could have that new hat.

It all happened so suddenly. Poole saw a tandem come around the corner of the street with a solitary man riding on the front seat. It pulled up at the kerbside next to the policewoman and a brief exchange of words took place. By the light of the chip shop window, Constable Poole recognised the cyclist as the man he had been told to arrest. Just to be sure, he checked off the description.

"Convict's outfit, with broad black arrows on a light background. Black mask and gangster's trilby hat. That's got to be my man."

He stood up on his pedals, poised ready to leap into life and pursue the tandem. But he held back as Mavis appeared to hesitate before she got onto the back seat of the cycle.

"Wait for it...Wait for it...Patience." Poole told himself. "Let him pick his floozy up for his nefarious purposes. Then I've got 'em both. My promotion will be in the bag."

The tandem, bearing a convict on the front seat

and a policewoman seated behind him, moved off from the kerb and rolled along the High Street. Poole shot from his hiding place and pedalled like fury in hot pursuit. He lacked the police siren to announce his presence but he did the best he could by imitating the sound with his mouth.

"He haw, he haw, he haw..." he brayed like a demented donkey as he closed in on the suspects.

George Willis heard the warning sound. He turned off his bicycle lights to aid his getaway, and steered down a darkened side street, stepping on the pedals as hard as he could. He knew to get caught in those circumstances would be the end of his career. Kerb crawling was a criminal offence. Ruin stared him in the face! Realising his only hope was to shake off his pursuer in the dark, he shouted over his shoulder to his passenger.

"Pedal like hell, Mavis. For God's sake move your legs!"

Miss Peabody was no sprint-racing cyclist neither was her uniform designed for such vigorous exercise. The narrow skirt rode up over her hips. Her white thighs and bare bottom flashed like twin beacons in Poole's front light, making it obvious which way they were going.

Constable Poole was a younger and fitter man than George Willis and his promotion spurred him on.

He drew alongside the tandem and shouted for them to stop.

"In the name... of the law...I order you to halt," he panted.

"Get stuffed." George yelled back at him, changing down a gear and surging forward.

In desperation Poole drew out his truncheon and rammed it into the flashing steel spokes of the tandem's front wheel.

There was a metallic sound like a harp being played with a sledgehammer. The tandem's rear wheel left the tarmac as it cartwheeled into the air. Mavis screamed as she flew over George's head and landed in the hedge, her skirt hem now up to her waist and her black nylon legs waving frantically in the moonlight, resembling a black and white victory sign.

George fell on the tarmac in a crumpled heap. The tandem landed on top of him knocking all the breath out of him.

I arrest you for kerb crawling, for being a convict on the run, for picking up that young lady for your illicit purposes, for driving without due care and attention on the highway, for breaking the speed limit and failing to show lights...Oh yes! And for trying to evade a police officer in the normal execution of his duty." Poole triumphantly clamped the handcuffs on his victim before he could recover.

George just groaned.   For once in his life the Lord of the Manor was speechless.

Chapter Twenty Three

Oswald, oblivious to the chase in the High Street, let himself into the chemist shop and descended the stairs to his underground laboratory. He went carefully, dodging the pheasants hung above the cellar stairs, where he'd left them to go high.

"I must persuade Lydia to cook me a game pie from those birds," He reminded himself, as he screwed up his empty chip paper and pitched it expertly up the steps into the shop waste bin.

Down below the shop he had made an experimental apparatus from the spare kettle. His aim was to produce wet weather on a large scale, not just to produce a storm in a bottle. Judging by the fine day he had produced for the town fete, he was really getting to grips with weather magic. Fine weather brewing was easy. Making rain to order, and controlling the amount that fell, might be more difficult.

"I need to give it a more stringent test than a

storm in a glass bottle." The Wizard muttered to himself. "Let's see? What sort of precipitation shall I go for? Snow? Not in summer. That might ruin some of the farmers' crops and I'm in enough trouble already, with all those damn rats! A good old full scale thunder storm would be alright though"

He set to mixing his potions and processing them in his test tubes. Finally, satisfied with the results, he corked the tubes and picked up his stainless steel weather machine. All was ready for a trial run.

"I just need to get out into the open air. I need plenty of space." Oswald always talked to himself when he was excited.

The Wizard gathered up all his bits and pieces and took them upstairs. He had difficulty carrying it all in his arms. As he ran up the steps, he accidentally bumped his head on a brace of game birds, dislodging several fat juicy maggots, which wriggled down the back of his shirt collar, but he was so engrossed in his plans he ignored the discomfort.

"What I need is a bag to hold some of this. I can't manage all this stuff in my two hands." He checked the back room and found Malcolm's cricket bag. He tipped out the bat and balls onto the floor and filled the holder with his own gear.

Once he was out of the shop and into the town, carrying his brother's cricket bag, he made for the public gardens. He had decided that a localised downpour over the park would do the least damage.

"Why don't I set this apparatus up on the covered bandstand? I can shelter there from the storm, while I make my observations," he muttered aloud.

Oswald crept stealthily through the deserted gardens in the half-light, and installed himself in the centre of the grassy play area, right next to the town bandstand.

Peter Piper made his telephone call to the police station then sprinted on his well-oiled legs into town. He deliberately chose not to overtake the tandem, staying back out of sight, but he made sure he was close enough to witness the success of his plans.

Once Constable Poole had arrested George Willis and his companion, the clown knew he was free for the rest of that night, to do what he had planned. There would be no official interference that evening, for he had rightly calculated that the admission of so important a person as George Willis to jail, would keep the local law occupied until the morning.

The clown made for the largest open space he could find, well away from the river and the rats. There he stretched himself out on his back, hidden in a flowerbed among the Red Hot Pokers. He unzipped his codpiece and unfurled the aerial, knowing it would go unnoticed among the tall flower spikes in the dark. Once his aerial was erected, he sent his radio signals up into the night sky and out into the town. By sheer coincidence, but for similar reasons of privacy, Peter Piper had chosen to use the local park; the very same place as the wizard.

Oswald set up his experiment and recited his magic spells, oblivious to the faint oscillating transmissions going out from the nearby flowerbed. By midnight both the clown and the Wizard were having success, in their different ways.

At the Dog in a Doublet, Lydia Postlethwaite had locked up the public house for the night and had taken herself upstairs to bed. She took her usual shower and poured herself a stiff nightcap before turning in. She was just falling into her first refreshing sleep when she had a most vivid dream.

Peter Piper appeared at the foot of her bed. She recognised him instantly. He was dressed in his black and white clothes with the three-cornered jester's hat on his head, but with one unusual addition. Funny, the landlady thought, I've never seen him with a flute in his hand.

The clown beckoned her to get up.

"Follow me, Lydia. I am the Lord of the Dance." The vision placed the flute between his lips and started to play a haunting tune. The melody proved irresistible. She rose from her bed, still fast asleep, and tripped lightly after the figure in her dream.

Lydia went down the stairs and out of the front door, into the empty streets, clad only in a diaphanous nightdress, which hid none of her famous tattoo from anyone who happened to be passing by. She did not realise that the huntsmen pictured racing down the twin hills of her breasts, the hounds skirting her navel and the fox's brush curling up her belly, were on display for the world to see. It was fortunate no one was about at that very early hour.

With both arms outstretched, like any self-respecting sleepwalker, she made for the park, following the haunting music of the imaginary flautist.

Malcolm Gotobed had gone to bed early with a headache. The excitement and stress of the fete had been too much for him. As he told his wife. "Conducting the choir was a joy. But that altercation with that blaspheming clown has really upset me. I don't know what the world is coming to. The choir heard all his swearing before the vicar and I could usher them away."

He and his wife took a mug of malted milk to their respective beds, started to watch a recording of Songs of Praise and were both sound asleep by ten o'clock.

As the town hall clock struck half past midnight,

Malcolm's wife was awakened from her first deep sleep by the sound of her husband walking along the landing and down the stairs. Dressed only in his paisley pyjamas and his slippers, he walked along the hall, unlocked the front door, and walked out of the house, his arms outstretched before him in classic sleepwalker's pose.

Freda Gotobed pulled on her dressing gown and rushed onto the landing. She knew better than to shout and wake him, fearing the sudden shock might kill him. When she heard the front door open and close behind him, she dressed and hurried down the stairs to follow her husband. But by the time she got to the front door, he was already out of the house and lost from sight. She hadn't a clue which way he had gone. As she stood in the open doorway, unsure what to do next, their baby cried from the nursery above. She burst into tears, slammed the front door shut and rushed upstairs to comfort the baby.

Five minutes later, with baby in her arms she decided to call for help.

"I'll phone Oswald. He'll know what to do."

She punched the telephone numbers in panic, but Malcolm's brother did not pick up his receiver.

"Oh God! What can I do now?" She broke down in tears again, and sat on the bottom step of the stairs, rocking the baby in her arms.

Mavis Peabody had just fallen into an exhausted sleep when she started to dream of the clown. She was entertaining her landlord that evening, keeping him sweet by supplementing her rent in kind. He had made sure he got his money's worth.

Mavis had fallen asleep with her back turned towards the chip shop owner, to avoid the smell of stale oil and fish, which always seemed to cling to his body. When she heard the clown's voice in her dreams, she shot out of bed. Her sleeping partner snored on. Nothing short of a police raid or the fire brigade would have disturbed him. She slipped out of her flat and sleepwalked towards the park, wearing nothing but a smile, which was all she ever wore in bed. Her pale figure trotted along the deserted pavement, brazenly displaying all her wares.

Michael Flannegan had left the Dog in a Doublet in a drunken state and hadn't managed to stagger all the way back to his digs. He collapsed onto a bench seat at the entrance to the public park and fell fast asleep. His loud snoring in the open air, disturbed no one but the roosting birds. When his call came from the clown he was out for the count. It was only the insistent voice of the figure in his dreams and the fact that he seemed to be offering a free pint of Guinness that eventually persuaded the Irishman to try to make a move.

"I'm coming. Just give me time to get my legs into gear and I'll be there." He made very slow progress into the park, falling down at every other step, but such was the power of the jester in his dream and the pull of a free drink, he kept getting up and continually trying again.

George Willis was spending an uncomfortable night in the police cells. He'd been most unhelpful when he was questioned. When it was explained that he had telephoned the station and shopped himself, he lost his temper and tried to strangle Constable Poole. He was locked up in the care of the night shift constable.

The Chief Constable received his call at about half past midnight. In his troubled sleep, the cell door seemed to spring open and the pied clown came in.

"Follow me Mr Policeman. I will save you."

George rose from his pallet and strode blindly towards the locked door. He hit his head on the iron bars and knocked himself out. That was as far as he went that night.

Constable Poole had gone home with a lot on his mind. He had arrested an escaped convict on the orders of his own Chief Constable, only to find he had taken the Chief Constable himself into custody. In normal circumstances he would have turned a blind eye to the events of the evening but George Willis was most abusive. The chief had even threatened to kill him.

Poole was in a fix. He wasn't sure what to do. He knew the chief would sack him if he got a chance. If he pressed charges on George Willis he would be fighting the old boys network, so he had to make the charges stick. Would anyone believe him when he explained what had happened that night? He realised he was the only witness to the original phone call and the subsequent chase and arrest. In desperation he decided to phone the assistant chief constable, an ambitious man who had his eyes on George Willis' job.

"Good man, Poole. It does look as if our dear chief has gone off the rails. Must have been a brainstorm. Perhaps he's been working too hard? Keep him locked up for his own good until I can get back to you."

"But he says this will cost me my job, sir. When he gets out he's going to throw the book at me."

"Nonsense, acting sergeant Poole. I'll see to it that nothing affects your position. You are a valuable asset to me...I mean to the force. You are the only police witness to his strange behaviour. You will be needed to testify. I will assume all his responsibilities from now on. Report directly to me, my man."

When he got home, Poole told his wife all about

the problem. He was so worried about his job, she had suggested he took one of her mild sleeping pills to help him relax. He had gone to bed, finally succumbing to sleep from sheer mental exhaustion. She took two of the pills and went out like a light.

Constable Poole's call from the clown came at the same time as his neighbour, Fred Hinman. The old fellow lived in a bungalow in the same quiet cul-de-sac. The two men met in their sleep and strode purposefully towards the park, looking like a pair of large storybook elves, as both of them wore nightshirts and pointed nightcaps.They were not a particularly good matching pair of elves, for the old man wore long red flannel and the constable had a short blue number decorated with fluffy bunnies.

Theo Willis stirred in his sleep when the vision of Peter Piper appeared at his bedside. "I'm coming. Hang on a minute," the antique dealer shouted in his sleep.

His wife woke up the instant she heard him speaking.

Theo repeated his shout. "I'm coming. Hang on a minute." Then rose from his bed and started rummaging in his wardrobe looking for his outdoor clothes.

His wife was shocked. "He's dreaming about that damn girl again. I'll put a stop to him. He might dream he's coming, but he's going nowhere!" She took the wax seal from its hiding place and hurriedly attached it across his bedroom door.

Theo, dressed in a tweed sports jacket over his silk pyjamas, collapsed against the inside of his bedroom door and snored there until morning.

Vickie Giles stirred in her sleep at her parents' farmhouse, far out in the fen. She had gone to bed early and was dreaming about Blackie. She imagined her lost black cat, had just crawled into her open window when it changed colour and turned into a black and white animal. Vickie sat up in bed and was holding out her arms to the creature, when she noticed it had Punch and Judy puppets on its front paws. Suddenly the cat changed into the clown she had seen at the brownie party.

"What are you doing here?" she asked.

"I need the Brownies help in town. Get out of bed and come down to the park in Runford."

The message was so compelling, Vickie slipped on the tracksuit she wore for gymnastics, and climbed out of her bedroom window. With her eyes wide open but still dreaming, she started to jog towards Runford.

At the end of the farm track she turned onto the main road and ran alongside a ditch which skirted the field where her father kept the pigs. Within a few minutes her regular footfalls were augmented by a gentle padding sound as a giant black cat joined her on the journey. The two figures ran on into the night. Vickie and Blackie were together again.

Runford is several miles away from the Giles farm. It would have taken Vickie several hours to jog into town, nevertheless she jogged on doggedly, hoping she would make it in time. The big cat followed at her heels.

Tina Stothard had a cold. She had gone to bed early with a hot lemon drink and had taken an antihistamine tablet, so she slept like a log. When the call from the clown came to her, she was dreaming about the time she and Oswald had seen the Black Panther. Oswald told her to hang onto his back as he chased the imaginary big cat across the fields on his motorcycle. Tina wrapped her arms tightly around her pillow.

"Get off the motorbike and walk into town." Oswald changed into Peter Piper and ordered her off the pillion seat.

Tina did as she was asked. She put her overcoat over her silk pyjamas, slipped on her outdoor shoes and walked towards the centre of town, a paper handkerchief held permanently over her running nose.

The clown lay on his back in the flowerbed looking up at the clear night sky with his eyes faintly glowing in the dark. Above him he noted a distant shadowy form, which blotted out some of the stars. He smiled at this first sign of his success. At last they were coming for him.

Completely unaware of these events, Oswald Gotobed concentrated on his weather magic, putting his heart and soul into the wet spell. He had been preparing for several days for this experiment and wanted desperately to succeed. He poured the ingredients from the test tubes into the old kettle, then closed his eyes and recited the Red Indian rain making chant, over and over again. At the same time he visualised the results he wanted to achieve. The brown fumes from his stainless steel weather-maker, spiralled lazily up into the cool night air, carrying his incantation skywards with them.

Eventually the High Wizard's positive thinking bore fruit. A gentle breeze sprung up over the park and small clouds began to gather over the bandstand. Oswald felt the sudden movement of air and the coolness of the wind as it gathered force about him. He smiled at his success and redoubled his efforts. Finally, with a loud clap of thunder, it began to rain.

Peter Piper, lying among the perennials, felt the first drops of rain on his face. He frowned and peered up into the sky, looking for the dark shadow he expected to see there, but only thick black storm clouds filled his field of view. There was a clap of thunder and a small bolt of lightning struck his aerial. He hastily rolled it down.

"This will never do! The weather forecast was fine. I must have good visibility. That's why I chose to summon them to collect me and my specimens on a clear night."

"Sure, but you can't rely on the English weather. Didn't the TV weather girl say it would be a fine night. That kind of forecast was sure to mean rain," the Punch puppet told him.

"I'll have to cancel the arrangement." The clown made a snap decision to call off the rendezvous for that night.

All over town, scurrying rats and sleepwalking humans stopped in their tracks. Like pale ghosts when the first rays of dawn appear, the locals abandoned their journeys to the park and turned back for their homes.

Lydia Postlethwaite sighed in her sleep, pirouetted on the newly cut park grass and trotted back to the Dog in a Doublet.

Malcolm, still soundly sleeping, walked back to his home and let himself in by the front door. He completely surprised his wife who was still sitting on the stairs, sobbing to herself and rocking their baby back to sleep. She put the sleeping child back in its cot, led her husband upstairs and tucked him up in his bed, where she lay with her arms entwined firmly around his neck, thankful that he had come to no harm and was back with them.

Constable Poole returned with Fred Hinman. He saw the old man to his front door then returned to his own bed, unnoticed. An earthquake would not have awakened his wife that night.

Most of the Runford sleep walkers returned unharmed to their beds, but one or two of them had problems.

Mavis Peabody was unfortunate. She disturbed her landlord as she crept back between the black silk sheets. He turned over and put his arms around her.

"Did I tell you how much I love you?" he whispered into her ear, his voice bleary with sleep.

She had to pay her rent all over again.

Vickie Giles hesitated when she received the message to go back home. It seems such a shame to have come so far, then go back without meeting the clown again. She sighed in her sleep before she turned and began the run back home. The cat heard the sigh and tried to comfort her by brushing itself against the girls legs, but being very large Blackie misjudged the movement and nearly knocked her off balance.

Vickie reached out in her sleep and stroked the cat's back.

"There you are, Blackie!" She grinned with pleasure at being reunited with her lost pet. "Follow me back home and I'll give you a saucer of milk." Vickie trotted home with her dark companion at her heels. When she had climbed back through her open bedroom window, she tiptoed downstairs to the kitchen to raid the fridge for milk.

As Vickie poured the milk into a saucer she woke up. At first she was disorientated, but then she remembered what she was doing in the kitchen and why. She recalled that Blackie was out in the yard waiting to be fed, just like old times. Vickie switched on the kitchen light and unbolted the back door. She stepped out into the yard, the saucer of milk held out in her hand.

"Come on Blackie. Here kitty-kitty." Even though Blackie was a wild farm cat, she responded to Vickie's voice and jumped up to get at the milk.

"Dad! Dad! Help!" Vickie screamed into the night as she came face to face with the huge black cat. "Dad! It's the Black Panther!" The saucer fell to the yard and broke into a dozen pieces. The cat startled by the noise, backed away in fright.

Mr and Mrs Giles woke up in a panic. They could hear their daughter shouting for help, but they were not sure where her voice was coming from. Her father ran along the landing to her bedroom but found her bed empty and the window wide open.

"Dad! Help" Vickie stood in the yard, her legs paralysed with fear, shouting at the top of her voice.

Hearing that her cry for help came from outside the house, Bill put his head out of the window. He discovered his daughter was in the yard, below him. By the light from the open kitchen door he saw she was not alone. Standing immediately in front of her was a huge black shape with glowing green eyes. It was the big cat they'd been warned about!

"I'm coming, love! I'll get my gun." Bill flew down the stairs in a panic.

Blackie was further startled by the voice shouting from above her. She turned tail and ran off into the darkness.

By the time Bill Giles had grabbed his shotgun and reached his daughter, Vickie was standing alone, crying in the yard. He put his arms around her and took her indoors to her mother.

"What ever were you doing outside at this time of the night?" Mrs Giles asked

"I must have been dreaming, mum." Vickie stopped sobbing and looked embarrassed at her feet. "I thought Blackie had come back to us." She tried to recall what had actually happened to her, but no matter how she tried, she couldn't bring the details back to mind. She realised sheepishly, that she was dressed in her track-suit and had running shoes on. "I must have dressed in my sleep. I'm sorry mum. I don't know what I was thinking about."

Bill Giles came in from checking the yard and the livestock. He had his shotgun resting over his arm.

"No sign of it. That panther was certainly in the yard when I looked out of Vickie's bedroom window, but it's gone now. No wonder the poor kid was frightened." He shook his head in amazement at her lucky escape. "Let that be a lesson young lady. No more gallivanting about outside at night; especially while that big cat's about." He put his arm around his wife and daughter and ushered them both back to bed. "It'll be a good thing when Blackie does show up again. Our daughter must be very worried about that cat, to start having nightmares about it."

Tina Stothard was trotting through the market place when the orders to go to the park were reversed. She stopped outside the chemist shop and hesitated. A bout of sneezing overtook her in the cool night air and she woke up with a start.

"Good God! Where am I?" She was amazed to find herself standing in front of Gotobed Brothers front door with a single paper tissue in her hand.

"I must have thought I was shopping for another box of paper handkerchiefs and some more cold tablets." She shivered and pulled her coat tightly round her. It was then she realised she had only her pyjamas on underneath and it was the middle of the night. She ran back to her home in a panic. Luckily she met no one on the way.

Michael Flannegan, was the one exception who did not make it back to his bed. The Irishman collapsed onto the grass verge as soon as he received his instruction to stop. He was still there, slightly damp and snoring loudly, when the park keeper checked the area next morning.

Oswald waited in the shelter of the bandstand for the rain to ease off, before he went home to his bed. He was very pleased with his night's work. All the sleepwalkers had gone before he left the park. Even Michael was fast asleep and out of sight behind one of the herbaceous borders. Oswald was completely ignorant of the problems he had caused the clown and unaware of the trouble he had saved several of his friends and neighbours.

Peter Piper was disappointed at his failure to obey his masters' orders and make contact. He made his way back to his lodgings by an entirely different route. At the Dog in a Doublet, he let himself into the pub and went straight to his room, where he sat down under the bedroom light. He took off his jester's hat and stroked his bald head as he considered his next move.

"Begorra! But I've no choice now. It's too late tonight. I'll have to try again, that I will. I'll try the next fine night and the one after that and the one after that. I'll try every fine night until I complete me mission."

Chapter Twenty Four

On Sunday Gotobeds' chemist shop was closed for normal business but they undertook dispensing duty from noon until one o'clock, opening the store for dealing with prescriptions and selling urgent medicines. There was always a demand for hangover cures, pregnancy tests and life saving surgical appliances, like condoms and baby's dummies, as well as the occasional urgent prescription. Oswald and Malcolm did this work together for it was normally a busy hour. As was usual for a Sunday duty, the shop emptied and business slackened off as one o'clock approached.

"Are you sickening for something, Malcolm? I noticed Freda has telephoned you three times in the last hour to check if you were alright. You've hardly said two words to me all rota and you look decidedly peaky."

"I had a bad night. In fact I haven't even been to early communion today. I slept in."

"Oh dear! Not been to church yet? That sounds serious. I told you not to take those Ginseng pills home to your wife. You'll never satisfy her now. I bet you've been at it all night!" Oswald enjoyed making his straight-laced brother feel uncomfortable. Malcolm and Freda had been married for twenty years and had produced a daughter, but Oswald still had his doubts about their love life.

Malcolm ignored the sarcasm. "I had a nightmare and I walked out of the house in my sleep."

"Not another bad dream? Where did you go? Over to the flat above the chip shop? If Mavis Peabody was at home, I bet it wasn't a dry dream!"

Malcolm shook his head in despair. "I'm not joking, Oswald. Freda assures me I was gone from my bed for half an hour. I'm afraid I went out into the street, dressed only in my paisley pyjamas. I've been dreading this would happen, after that first time"

"Well I'll be damned! The Lincolnshire flasher strikes again!"

Malcolm ignored his brother's jokes and carried on explaining. "I dreamed about that black and white clown who came into the shop. You know, the one you claimed had tried to rob us."

"No claim about it, brother! He nearly got away with forty quid of our hard earned takings. If I hadn't been here you would have handed it over to him."

"Well, I think that episode must be preying on my mind. I dreamed that fellow was calling me to meet him. It seems I got up in my sleep and walked into town, even though it was dark."

Oswald, in spite of his off-hand manner, was really very concerned about his brother. "Why don't you try a bottle of that new tonic wine from the stockroom and treat yourself to an alcoholic night cap before you go to bed. Take some of those vitamin pills that cure everything. We've got a thousand of them on the dispensary shelf."

Malcolm was touched at his concern. "Do you think that will help, Oswald?"

"Drink the whole bottle of tonic wine. I guarantee you'll not walk down those stairs until the morning. If then."

After the dispensing duty, Malcolm went straight home to his meat, two veg and Yorkshire pudding, prepared by his doting wife. Oswald went to the Dog in a Doublet for a bachelor's liquid lunch and another chance to chat up the landlady.

Sunday lunchtime in the pub was always quiet. The younger crowd had shot their bolts on Saturday night. Even the ones who had rolled out of bed that early and could stomach another lager, were in a subdued mood, only sipping at half pints. It was not unusual to hear complaints about the loud noise of the darts thumping into the treble twenty or the pensioners clicking the dominoes and blowing their noses at full volume. The jukebox was turned off. Playing music was out of the question on a Sunday lunch time in the Dog in a Doublet.

Michael Flannegan was made of stronger stuff. He always called in on Sundays for an energetic game of dominoes and a top up with Guinness.

"Afternoon, Michael…and you Constable Poole." Oswald called his greeting across the bar to the two domino players. He ordered his pint from the landlady and was about to take it to a secluded corner table when Lydia reached out and grabbed his arm to restrain him.

"Can you spare me a minute, Os?"

Noting the serious expression on her face, he sat down on the nearest bar stool and sipped his beer. He eyed her thoughtfully. She didn't look at all her normal, cheery self. Perhaps she was ill and needed some advice, or maybe some loving sympathy? He was hopeful of the latter. Perhaps he could tentatively suggest bed for the afternoon?

"What's up, Lydia?" He wiped the white smear of froth from his upper lip.

"I want a private word with you. I'm not well." She looked suitably pained.

"Too much booze? It's an occupational hazard.

You'll have to stop accepting freebies from your customers."

"No. It's nothing to do with that. I'm not sleeping properly and I've seen the doctor about it, but last night I had a terrible nightmare."

"You and my brother, both."

"Oh! Is Malcolm not well?"

"According to him, at about 12.30 in the morning he dreamed that your lodger called him from his bed. He walked in his sleep into the town. Would you believe it? My straight laced brother flitting around Runford in the middle of the night, dressed like Wee Willy Winkie!"

The bar fell ominously silent at these comments. The energetic click of dominoes stopped instantly. Michael and the constable put down their beers and turned to stare open mouthed at the druggist.

"What have I said? They can't touch me for it can they?" Oswald swallowed hard at this unexpected attention. "Malcolm meant no harm; honestly! He didn't know what he was doing. I was only kidding when I called him the Lincolnshire flasher."

"I dreamed exactly the same dream." Lydia dropped her hand to her breast and whispered in shock.

"And me!"

"Me too!" Chorused the domino team.

"Get on with you, you're having me on." Oswald chuckled into his beer for he enjoyed a leg pull with the best of them. He turned to grin at the speakers, but meeting their serious faces and shocked expressions, he put down his glass and changed his tone.

"You mean it, don't you. Well I'll be damned! The doc mentioned an epidemic of sleepwalking. Malcolm's wife says he got out of bed and walked out of the house, dressed only in his pyjamas. She was left at home, holding the baby. He came back about an hour later, still fast asleep. His wife hasn't a clue where he went but he certainly left the street where they live because she lost sight of him from the house."

"Good God!" Lydia clasped her hands to her face in horror. "I dreamed I was walking into town, after Mr Piper appeared to me in my sleep. This morning I found all damp grass cuttings in my bed, and they were stuck between my toes. They weren't there when I showered last night. It was as if I'd been out in the park, in my bare feet on the newly cut grass!" She clutched at the bar to hold herself upright. "Now here you are telling me it wasn't just a nightmare and it actually happened!" She coloured up bright red as the full implications hit her. " But I only had on my flimsy nylon nightdress. It's very see through! Anybody I met would have seen everything!" She crossed her arms protectively over her breast and looked sheepishly around the bar at the other two sleepwalkers.

Oswald had seen her in that particular diaphanous nightdress and was dying to make some facetious comments about moonlit hunts with galloping horses and vanishing foxes, but seeing her ashen face, he thought better of it and stayed silent.

"Don't look at me! I didn't see you in your flimsies." PC Poole gulped. After a pregnant pause he added slowly. "Anyway... I sleep in a rather short nightshirt myself. My wife calls it a bum freezer! Hardly the sort of garment to wear for a walk about town."

Michael considered his position thoughtfully. "I left here after closing time, didn't I?"

"Yes, as usual." Lydia agreed.

"I woke up in a flower bed in the park this morning."

"Also as usual." Oswald quipped.

"Yes, but I do recall dreaming about that nice black and white clown that I saw in the Hole-in-the-Wall passageway. He was calling me to come to him in the park. When I woke up this morning I was on the grass in the park, wet through. There must have been quite a storm in the night."

Mention of the storm, jogged Oswald's memory. Without thinking he said. "Well if you all did sleepwalk, I didn't notice any of you in the park last night."

"What were you doing in the park? Did you have a dream as well?"

"Well, not exactly...I was doing some...er...observations for the...er...RUFS. Eclipses of the moon...and important things like that, you know." Hurriedly he finished his drink, made a lame excuse and left the bar for home.

As he walked along, his hands thrust deep into his trouser pockets, he was lost in thought. It struck him as peculiar that he knew of five unconnected local people, who all had the same dream. It was equally baffling that Peter Piper, the pied clown, was at the centre of each one.

Oswald reviewed his feelings about the clown as he went home. I disliked that fool from the very first time we met. He has a most unusual mind. I tried to see into his brain. It was unreadable, even to me. He has a lot to answer for. He tried to cadge forty quid from Malcolm. He tried it on with Lydia, buttering her up to get his own way. He made those funny noises, like a radio receiver, at the top of the fire station tower...and of course there was that business with the rats.

Oswald shuddered at the memory of the rats and unconsciously stroked his wrists. He wasn't sure how the rats fitted into the scenario but he was ready to think the worst of the jester.

Thoughts of the rats reminded him that Blackie, the Black Panther of Lincolnshire, was still on the loose. He grunted at this reminder of his own incompetence and put that problem to the back of his mind for the minute. He muttered to himself as he walked along.

"To top it all, Peter Piper talks to himself in different voices and plays with those glove puppets, he begged from Fred Hinman. He must be unhinged. I'll keep an eye out for him. Mind you, with any luck he'll be leaving us, now that the town fete is over,"

Chapter Twenty Five

Next morning Oswald took the day off from the pharmacy to sort out the problem of the Black Panther. He suspected the cat would have given birth by then and he feared the litter would be extra large kittens, like their mother. That meant there would be three or four dangerously large cats stalking the South Lincolnshire fens as soon as Blackie had weaned her family.

He went into the shop early, before Malcolm arrived for business, and prepared enough fresh shrinking potion to deal with Blackie and her whole family. He also dabbed a liberal drop of Australian Poppy perfume behind each ear, from the tester on the cosmetic counter, for he remembered selling a bottle of the cheap perfume to Vickie Giles and she was the only person the cat would trust.

Oswald decided to start his search on Will Giles land, hoping that the cat would stick to its familiar home territory. He went straight to the lane overlooking the copse where he had last sighted the animal. Unfortunately he found he was not the only one there. He was not pleased with the company he found.

"Hello, My Gotobed. What are you doing here?" Tina had arrived there before him, and she had brought two other members of the Runford Natural History Society with her.

"I happened to be passing by and stopped to see if that panther was still around. And you?"

"I'm doing the same thing. Gerald and Ken have experience of watching big cats in Africa. Gerald has actually wrestled with one, just as you did." Tina's eyes shone with admiration as she referred to this feat. "They will bw able to provide a positive identifiction for me. If we are lucky enough to see it."

Oswald was not happy to hear this. Blackie was an overgrown domestic cat. Then the fat would be in the fire. Will Giles and the other farmers would be after him for compensation for their lost livestock. He tried to put them off waiting.

"Surely you don't expect it to have stayed around here? Especially after that brush we had with it?"

"They are creatures of habit." Ken assured him. "Anyway, we think we caught sight of something suspicious leaving the copse just as we arrived. We think we saw it slinking along the drain on the far side. We intend to wait here and keep observation until it returns. We are downwind of it here..." He sniffed pointedly at Oswald..."You can't be too careful what scent you wear on these wild life expeditions."

Oswald wasn't pleased with this reference to the Australian Poppy or the presence of these intruders. There was no way he could sneak over to the copse while they were sytanding guard. He would have to resort to subterfuge again and use his vanishing spells.

"I wish you luck then. I must be off." He kicked the Triumph motorbike into life and drove off in the direction of Runford. Once out of sight around a bend in the road, the Wizard cut the ignition and hid his bike behind a hedge.

Oswald sneaked back towards the group of mammal watchers. They were engrossed in their cat watch and chatting quietly about big cats in Africa. Just before he came into their view, he recited both invisibility spells. He and his feet vanished into thin air.

Being invisible, it was easy for the wizard to walk unseen past Tina and her friends and climb the gate into the field adjacent to the copse. His perfume was not so easy to hide.

"There's that awful smell again. I'm sure that old chap was wearing perfume. What a ponce!" Ken sniffed the air and commented to Tina.

Oswald was seething at this remark. He didn't even bother to stay quiet once he was in the grass field. He whistled tunelessly as he walked, hoping the sound would to give the watchers something else to think about.

"Did you hear that?" Tina held up a silencing finger and scanned the field with her binoculars.

"Got to be a Meadow Pipit, surely?" Ken said.

"No. It was a Skylark." Gerald was adamant.

Tina searched the field and the sky in vain.

Oswald, who was just within earshot of the twitchers, hooted like an owl to really set them thinking. "Bloody impostors!" He muttered to himself.

Once he came near the copse, Oswald slowed his pace and crept forward more carefully. He might have fooled those twitchers but Blackie would not be so easily hoodwinked. He took his time and worked his way towards the spot that he had seen the big cat use as a den.

At first Oswald was disappointed. There was no sign of the large black cat. It looked as if Tina was right when she said they had frightened Blackie away when they arrived.

Oswald stood very still and considered his next

move. He was in two minds whether to wait patiently until dusk, when he was certain the cat would return, or go back and return later in the day. As he stood and weighed up the possibilities, a faint sound from near his feet claimed his attention. He bent over and parted some thick tufts of dried vegetation, which had been deliberately scraped over a hollow in the ground.

Oswald was stunned. His search revealed three kittens sleeping at his feet. They were no ordinary kittens, but oversized ones! Blackie had had her litter only a few hours before. Even though their eyes were still tightly closed. Each was already as big as a fully-grown farm cat. He smiled at his find and fondled one of them under the chin. They were beautiful. Two of the kittens were jet black like their mother. The third one was pure white.

"You could become the famous Lincolnshire Snow Leopard." He mouthed the words to himself, feeling almost sorry he had to return the kittens to their proper size.

Oswald had come well prepared. From his pocket he took a feeding bottle of ready mixed baby milk with the reducing potion already added. He tickled the white kitten under its chin again to wake it up and he let it suckle from the bottle. When he had given a third of the milk to that kitten, he fed its siblings, each in turn. With a sigh of relief he realised he had completed the first part of his mission. The kittens would soon return to their proper size. Now came the hard part. How was he going to dose Blackie with the antidote? He was sure that the big cat would not leave her litter for long. She had probably gone hunting and would soon return. He put down the last kitten and moved away from them to wait for the mother to return.

Oswald had a long wait. For several hours he propped himself up against a tree in the middle of the copse. The inactivity made him feel sleepy and he nearly dozed off as the day grew warmer. Suddenly a pheasant flew up from the dyke side and he heard an unfamiliar noise from the perimeter of the trees. Was it Blackie returning to her kittens? He glanced over at the litter and was shocked to see they had already begun to shrink to a normal size. That was a disaster! Maybe their mother would not accept this change. She may even kill them! He jumped to his feet and moved towards the sound, hoping to intercept the cat before it saw the kittens.

Oswald didn't find Blackie, as he had expected. He discovered the scuffling sound was Gerald, the big game expert from the natural history society. The twitcher was crawling along the side of the drain towards the copse. By the amount of unnecessary noise the man was making, Oswald guessed he was hoping to frighten away any lurking big cat, long before he came face to face with it. An army could have moved more silently. Oswald chuckled to himself. Wrestled with big cats my foot, he's more frightened than a rabbit. He decided to have some fun at Gerald's expense.

Oswald sat down at the edge of the trees and waited for the naturalist to creep level with him. As Gerald nervously raised his head above the dyke side, straining his eyes and ears to check what was in the copse, Oswald jumped up and growled loudly.

There was no chance that Gerald could see what had made the noise so close to his left ear, because the Wizard was still invisible. The naturalist panicked and screamed. Oswald saw Tina and Ken leap up from their hiding place behind the hedgerow as Gerald broke cover and ran back to the road, as if the big cat was already snapping at his heels.

Oswald laughed aloud.

"Big game hunter my fat aunt. He's an impostor."

Soon after that little incident the trio of animal watchers left. They had made so much noise they realised there was no chance the cat would return. Oswald saw then pack up their things and drive of towards the town.

"Thank God for that! Now I can wait in peace

for Blackie to come back to her litter." He had solved one problem but he still wasn't sure how to tackle the big cat herself, when she eventually put in an appearance.

It was getting dusk when Oswald heard a muffled growl from across the field. He froze on the spot and held his breath. There it was again! The same unusual sound, but this time, much nearer! He opened the tin of cat food, stirred in the antidote and put it on the ground next to the kittens.

The big cat came into the copse, silent as a shadow, and was standing beside her litter before he even realised that she was there. She approached them soundlessly on her padded feet. Oswald knew she was suspicious of his presence by the way she kept looking over her shoulder and making small growling sounds, deep inside her chest. He stood absolutely still and watched.

Blackie inspected her shrunken babies and seemed suspicious of them. Finally, after sniffing them thoroughly, she settled down beside them but would not allow them to feed from her. Oswald realised he would have left his scent on the kitten but he was banking on the fact that Blackie was familiar with Australian Poppy perfume and not averse to it. She even sniffed once at the open tin of cat meat but she must have eaten recently because she chose to ignore it.

"Damn that!" Oswald forgot himself and cursed under his breath. It was a very quiet comment, but not quiet enough! The big cat leapt up from her litter and paced the ground, sniffing at the air. Thank God he had had the sense to wait downwind of her! But still she did not settle. Finally she stalked to the edge of the copse and started to drink water from the drain.

Oswald had a sudden flash of inspiration. He leapt to the kittens and scooped the meat from the tin with his bare fingers. Quickly he smeared the cat meat all over the kittens' fur. He had finished this task just as Blackie returned from her drink. She stopped and sniffed the air. Once again the familiar perfume allayed her fears.

When the cat settled down again beside her offspring, she sniffed at each one of them, exactly as Oswald had hoped. It was a painfully slow business for she was still unsettled and kept raising her head to sniff the air. He realised it was only her powerful mothering instinct, and the fact that she was used to the aroma of Vickie Giles perfume, that had kept her in the copse all this time. He watched with growing excitement as she spent time nuzzling each small furry bundle. If only she would lick off the cat food. If that happened, all he had to do was wait for her to leave, then creep away and go home.

By this time Oswald was getting cramp in his leg from standing still for so long. He put up with the discomfort for as long as he could, but finally he had to move his foot to ease the pain. That slight movement was enough. Immediately, Blackie raised her head and growled at him. It had grown dark by that time and even though she could not see him, her sense of smell and hearing had pinpointed his position. The cat stalked over towards him and sniffed at his invisible body. He felt the animal's nose press against the unseen material of his jacket. She sniffed along his body towards his head.then she nuzzled his face in the dark, he knew she had found him out.

"Hello Blackie. Good little kitty." Oswald spoke quietly to try to reassure her.

The big cat growled a low warning in her throat.

The Wizard was petrified at the closeness of the animal, but he kept assuring himself it was really only an overgrown farm cat. With a trembling hand, he reached out and tentatively stroked its good ear. The cat went rigid, frozen to the spot.

"Nice pussy. Good cat." Oswald soothed the animal for all he was worth. After what seemed an eternity, Blackie responded by licking his neck with her large rough tongue. He breathed a sigh of relief and turned to walk away.

The cat let him take one step towards freedom

then she pounced on him like a house cat playing with a mouse. Her large front paws hit him squarely between his shoulder. The impact brought him crashing to the floor of the copse. Oswald panicked. He thought his time had come. He curled into a ball to protect his face and prayed for deliverance. The cat pawed his back and rolled him over, then it stood on his chest and licked his face. Its jaws were so close he could feel her hot breath on his cheek. It took him several minutes to realise that Blackie only wanted to play with him. He eased himself slowly forward on his hands and knees, but every time he started to move the cat pounced on him as if it was playing with a rag mouse.

Oswald was bruised and battered by the playful animal, but no matter how he tried, he could not get away from her. As it grew dark and the moon came up over the fields he lay on the ground among the trees with the cat draped heavily across his stomach.

The kittens crawled over to join them. Blackie's warm body and the constant purring eventually lulled him into a fitful sleep.

At dawn, when the sun's first rays shone onto Oswald's face, he woke up with a start.

"God I'm cold! Must have kicked off the duvet in my sleep." He reached down to pull up his bed covers and grabbed hold of the giant cat's fur.

Blackie, not used to being disturbed in her sleep, leapt into the air and growled! The kittens squealed. All hell was let loose! It was a rude awakening for them all. Memory flooded back to the Wizard. He sat up and opened his eyes, afraid of what he might find. He found Blackie was gone and her three tiny kittens were crawling on his lap, mewing loudly for their breakfasts.

Oswald uncurled himself and got painfully to his feet.

"God, but I am stiff! I'm getting a bit too old for this boy scout stuff!" He looked around at the wet bushes surrounding him and realised he had slept under the relative dryness of a tree while it had rained during the night.

The kittens continued their pleading cries for food. He realised their mother had refused to suckle them as she had not recognised those diminutive bundles of fur as her own litter. This was yet another disaster he had not anticipated. It was all his doing. Now he had the lives of Blackie's kittens on his conscience to add to all his other problems.

He looked down at the fluffy bundles and spoke to them.

"I'll have to take you home with me until I can return your mother to her normal self." Ignoring the smell of cat food, he placed the three mewing kittens into his jacket pockets, Oswald walked back across the fields to his motorbike.

"I suppose I should be pleased you are all back to your original size, but I'm certain I've not heard the last of the saga of the Lincolnshire panther!"

On the far side of the copse, the big black cat sniffed the air and strained her ears to hear the cries of her kittens.

Chapter Twenty Six

On Monday and Tuesday nights it rained. It was a natural occurrence and nothing to do with the Wizard's weather magic, but the wet weather combined with his problems with the Black Panther kept him away from the park. There was nothing to be gained by conjuring up wet weather when nature had already provided it, and the added complication of magically making good weather just to ruin it again, didn't seem worth his while. He spent the evening playing with the three kittens and filling the fridge with baby milk for their feeds.

Peter Piper was also thwarted by the cloudy skies. He kept to his room while it was overcast. To pass the time he took off his hat and crouched under his reading light. He was praying for a fine night so that he could try again to complete his mission. Time was running out for him.

On Wednesday, the BBC weatherman forecast a clear fine night with perhaps a little drizzle by morning. Oswald decided it was an ideal opportunity to visit the park once again to practice his rain making skills. He fed the kittens their milk with an eye dropper before he left for the shop.

Peter Piper was also pleased to hear the promise of good conditions. He was bored with waiting. His memory was bursting with the information he had collected. His mission was all but over. There was no point in prolonging his visit.

"Sure, but we are leaving tonight. Pack your bags and take your sun cream," Punch observed, happily.

Judy answered him. "I'm due for me holidays. I only hope the brewery remembers to send a relief manager to look after the pub."

Oswald went back to his laboratory after the shop had closed. He needed to prepare his experiment. As it grew dark he crept to the park, and installed himself on the bandstand with his stainless steel apparatus, just as he had on the previous occasion. This time he remembered to take his mobile telephone, in case Freda needed to contact him about his brother. Oswald had promised faithfully to be available if Malcolm took off in his sleep again.

"This is going to be another long and interesting night," he muttered, as he set up his apparatus. "I will produce rain first, then a thunder storm and finally clear skies by early morning. That is the exact opposite of the forecast given on the TV. That way I can be sure I caused the weather and it was not just a coincidence. If I succeed it will be one in the eye for the meteorology office. They are always saying how good they are at predicting the weather with their newfangled satellites. Let's hear them explain tonight's weather."

Just after midnight the clown ambled into the park and settled down in the flowerbed, just as he had before. He undid his codpiece, erected his aerial and started to transmit his homing signals. His telescopic aerial stood erect among the Redhot Pokers and Delphiniums, well camouflaged by those tall blooms. Once he established contact and confirmed the rendezvous was on for that night, he turned his attention to the people he had mesmerised. They must be available in the park when they were needed. His masters would be pleased with him and delighted with his collection of humans.

Over on the bandstand, Oswald recited his Red Indian chants and made his magic passes. He did not see the arrival of Peter Piper nor did he hear the high pitched tones of the clown's transmissions. Some other folk in the Runford area were not so lucky. They certainly got the clown's message.

At the riverside, numerous rats crawled out of

their holes and sniffed the night air. Whiskers twitched and noses wrinkled with pleasure at the magical sound wafting on the breeze. They all headed in the direction of the town's park. Drawn by the music of the clown's transmitter, the rodents scrambled up the banks and ran along the gutters at the roadside towards the haunting music.

At the Dog in a Doublet, Lydia Postlethwait had just fallen asleep, exhausted from a busy evening hosting a successful happy hour. She rose from her bed, clad only in a thin transparent nightdress. With both arms held out before her, she walked down the stairs, through the empty bar and out into the night. This time she took the precaution of putting on her slippers. Lydia walked into the centre of town, along the footpath. Beside her, in the gutter, dozens of rats ran in the same direction. If she had been awake and aware of her escort, the landlady would probably have screamed and fainted, but she was blissfully unaware of her travelling companions.

Malcolm sat up in his sleep. His wife had insisted he attach a bell on a ribbon to his big toe. The alarm sounded. She realised with a start what was happening and tried to take his outstretched hands and guide him back into bed, but he wouldn't be persuaded.

"I must ring Oswald for help." Freda muttered to

herself, as she followed her sleepwalking husband down the stairs.

"Come on, Oswald. Do answer me. You promised. Come on!" She let her brother-in-law's telephone ring out for ages but no one picked it up. By this time her husband had let himself out of the house and was striding purposefully into town, bound for the public park. Freda panicked and thumped the telephone with her clenched fist.

"If it's so good to talk, as they claim on those TV adverts," she bellowed. "Why won't anyone listen to me?" Then she remembered Oswald had a mobile phone. She rushed back up the stairs for her handbag and rifled through it to find his number. Unfortunately this noise woke the baby.

Acting sergeant Poole was on night duty at the police station. He had eaten a large bag of chips for his supper and was relaxing behind the reception desk, resting his eyes and reading inside his eyelids at the end of a busy shift. Earlier that day he had taken George Willis, the disgraced Chief Constable, to the county prison at Lincoln to await a preliminary hearing. At that late hour things were very quiet at Runford police station. Sergeant Poole soon fell asleep and began to dream.

'Poole of the Yard' they would call him, when he had proved to the world how good a detective he really was. The humdrum routine of arresting speeding motorists and cautioning shop lifting grannies was not for him. His dreams included the solving of several baffling Sherlock Holmes cases and some of the famous Agatha Christie mysteries. He was surprised when the clown appeared in one of his sleeping fantasies.

"Follow me Superintendent Poole. Your sleuthing skill is needed in the park."

Poole pulled on his helmet and strode purposefully out of the police station, leaving the desk unattended.

"Hello, hello, hello," he muttered in his sleep. "I'm needed urgently in the park. Poole of Scotland Yard will solve it again."

As Malcolm hurried by the darkened chip shop, he was joined on his sleep walk by Mavis Peabody. Luckily he was unaware of the girl, for he was still fast asleep. Fortunately too, Freda was not following him, for Mavis always slept in the nude. She spent so much time taking her clothes on and off during her working hours, she considered it a waste of time putting night clothes on at bedtime.

She trotted along beside the Chemist, her brightly painted fingernails outstretched, like two bunches of artificial holly berries. Her firm breasts jiggled in time with her footsteps and her well rounded buttocks, still glistening from the last customer and an application of Baby Oil, rotated like a pair of well oiled pistons. The erotic image was spoiled only by two things. Her hair, which was set in large mauve rollers, and a pair of large brown rats that ran at her feet.

Even though he was asleep, Fred Hinman knew he was getting too old for the sleepwalking lark. He took his bicycle from the shed and sleep-pedalled towards the park, still snoring loudly, completely ignoring the breeze up his nightshirt.

Michael Flannegan was already in the park, conveniently asleep under a vacant bench. The Irishman staggered to his feet, tore off his newspaper bedding and marched unsteadily towards the clown's signal. He sang snatches of his favourite Irish songs as he went.

Vickie Giles had a similar dream to the other victims. She got up and dressed herself in her track suit and crept out of her bedroom window. Down in the farmyard she had a sudden memory of the last time she had tried to jog into Runford to meet the clown. She realised it was much too far to run, so she took the Range Rover keys from the kitchen and backed the vehicle slowly out of the yard. She set off at a slow pace in a low gear.

Blackie, still searching for her lost family, stood at

the entrance to the farm and sniffed the air. She saw the Range Rover pass by and scented that Vickie was driving it. The big cat loped along the road after the car, keeping the rear lights always in view.

As she drove into Runford, still fast asleep but with her eyes open, Vickie stopped at her friend's houses and picked up some of the other mesmerised brownies. Others she stopped for at the roadside. Soon the car was full of dreaming young girls, some in brownie uniforms but many still in their night clothes. They sang campfire songs to pass the time as they travelled along.

Blackie followed at a distance, drawn by the faint scent of Australian Poppy and guided by the strains of Vickie's voice leading the singsong.

The car rolled into Runford and halted near the park. The girls disembarked and formed a crocodile behind Vickie Giles. They marched into the park in double file.

Tina Stothard, dressed in a pair if blue silk pyjamas, arrived on the scene at the same time as the Brownies. She fell in beside Vickie and led the pack on an organised sleep walk towards the play area.

Oswald started his spell-making routine. He mixed the ingredients in his converted kettle and was just beginning to recite the Red Indian chant when his mobile telephone rang out into the night. In the solitude of the park the telephone's insistent ring cut the air like a full peal of church bells. The Wizard cursed loudly and searched his pockets to locate the nuisance.

"Yes, Oswald Gotobed here. Who is it? What do you want?" He half expected it to be a patient with an urgent prescription, or the doctor himself, wanting an out of hours, tonic wine. He was taken by surprise when Freda's familiar voice screamed down the phone at him.

"It's Malcolm! He's gone walkabout again in his sleep. I'm stuck here with the baby and I don't know what to do."

"No, not again! Can't you keep him better occupied in bed?"

Freda snorted something down the phone, which Oswald couldn't quite catch, but from her tone he knew he'd overstepped the mark with his last question. He hastily changed the subject by asking. "Which way is he headed?"

"I don't know. I'm in my night clothes and I'm still in the house."

"Right. I'll come over and we can start a search." The Wizard pocketed his mobile and bent down to cover over his steel rain making apparatus with the cricket bag, confident it would be safe on the bandstand until he could return and start his experiment again. He was stooping over his experiment, closing the valves, when a rat ran over his feet. He hopped from one foot to the other, trying to avoid contact with the rodent.

"Not again! The whole bloody town is alive with them! I'll see the council first thing tomorrow…"

A voice barked out in the night, stopping Oswald in mid sentence. An unusual pink glow lit up the grass.

"Don't move! You are up to some mischief again, Mr Gotobed, or I'll be a leprechaun's uncle." The strange voice seemed to emanate from the depths of the pink glow.

Oswald turned around in surprise, looking for Michael Flannegan, whose voice he had recognised. He came eye to eye with Peter Piper, standing only a few yards away from him. Oswald gulped hard, shocked and amazed at the man's appearance.

The clown stood poised for action like a gunfighter. One hand was resting on his hip as if he carried a Colt 45. He had removed his funny hat and was now bare headed. Rainbows of coloured lights shone up into the darkness from his shiny bald scalp. For the first time, he had removed his pied costume to reveal a sleek body made of some matt metallic substance. The retractable aerial, which he had always secreted in his codpiece, now hung down towards the ground. He held it in his other fist like the handle of a strange metal detector.

From his body language and the tone of his voice, Oswald knew the creature meant business. He hesitated while he tried to make sense of the transformation. "You aren't a man at all, are you. You look like you're made of metal! What exactly are you?"

Peter Piper laughed a high mechanical laugh. "I am an advanced information gathering robot. I was sent here from another galaxy to spy on you humans."

Oswald frowned and shook his head in disbelief. "You had a bad knock on the head when you hit that juke box. You don't know what you're saying. A couple of aspirin and a day in bed will put you right."

The clown ignored his advice. "I came here five hundred years ago by your human reckoning. I beamed down to Hamelin Town in Brunswick to collect information for my masters. I was disguised as a medieval jester."

Oswald shook his head in disbelief.

The clown continued. "I was doing well in Hamelin until those stupid rats were attracted to my transmitter. Then the children started to follow me around and the Burgomaster set the town constables onto me." Peter Piper edged nearer to the wizard, all the time he was speaking.

"Rats! Of course, you attracted the bloody rats! It was your fault I got bitten at the fire station! You are the legendary Pied Piper of Hamelin!" Oswald was beginning to believe the robot and decided to play for time by trying to keep him talking while he thought of a way to escape. "Tell me, how did you get from Germany to here, and where have you been for the past five hundred years?"

"I stowed aboard a wine ship and came to Runford to escape the Burgomaster. But once here I ran into trouble with the lack of light. It was winter, you understand. My solar batteries ran out of energy. When I was helpless, your prior had me bricked up in a stone wall." As it spoke the robot eased its way ever closer to Oswald. He knew he couldn't hypnotise the Wizard easily, he had tried and failed at the pharmacy when they first met, but if he could get near enough he thought he could try to overpower him physically.

"Why the Irish voices?" Oswald started to step backwards, mirroring the robot's approach and preparing to run for his life.

Peter Piper ran out of patience.

"That is enough information for you, little wizard. You know too much already. It is time I dealt with you once and for all. I'll put a stop to your interference with the weather, for a start." The robot's eyes glowed deep red. Two sharp beams of visible energy shot from them, converging on the converted steel kettle, melting it instantly. The molten metal ran in bright rivulets, smouldering into the wooden floor of the bandstand, sending acrid wisps of smoke up into the night air.

Oswald choked on the fumes from the scorched wood and looked angrily at the charred remains of his weather spell. With all his work gone up in smoke, he shouted at the clown.

"Was that really necessary? I was only making a little storm with my weather magic."

"I understand everything now. You were here the other evening. It was you interfering with the weather and aborting my mission." This time there was no Irish brogue in the voice. There was no mistaking the metallic sound of the robot's voice box. The sound rose even higher, to a high manic pitch.

"You will be exterminated! Exterminate! Exterminate. You must not stop me tonight. My masters are on their way."

Oswald stared at his adversary in horror. The creature was surely going mad! Then hearing the faint tinkle of a bicycle bell, he lifted his gaze beyond the clown into the darkness surrounding them. He was very relieved to see shadowy figures moving towards them, across the park. There was constable Poole, Malcolm and Michael Flannegan, all converging on them. The sight of Lydia Postlethwaite in a billowing transparent nylon creation, and Mavis Peabody, completely in the nude, failed to register immediately. Suddenly Tina Stothard leading a crocodile of Brownies joined the others.

The new arrivals stopped in an arc a little way behind the clown. They showed no signs of hearing Oswald's cries but just stood in silence, frozen to the turf.

"Poole, arrest this lunatic! Malcolm, help me sort him out!" Oswald yelled.

No one moved. They stood rooted to the spot, deaf to Oswald's pleas.

"These people are my guests." The robot smiled cynically, his imitation human teeth flashing pearly white in his pink steel gums.

In desperation, Oswald made his move. He vaulted off the bandstand and dashed across the grass, hoping to dodge the robot and reach his brother. He covered only a few yards when he skidded on another rat and fell onto the ground. Before he could get up, the whole area was lit up, as if by daylight. From above him a huge beam of light played down on to the park, brighter than the floodlighting at a late night football fixture.

Oswald gasped in surprise and tried to look up towards the intense light, shielding his eyes with his hands. Above them he could just make out a vast circular shadow, like the underside of a giant bowler hat. It stood out black against the night sky. The hovering object was so wide it blotted out the moon and most of the stars. In the centre of the shadow, he could see a trapdoor, which was open towards the ground. From this opening a brilliant light shone down onto the park, illuminating everything.

"My masters have come for me and my specimens. My masters are here for me. My mission is over." The clown recited the explanation in his tinny robot voice. "My mission to planet Earth is completed at last. I have all the information they need and enough live human samples for all their experiments."

The awful truth hit the wizard! In that instant, he realised the clown was an alien machine, sent by some horrible denizens of deep space to gather humans, like a schoolboy might catch butterflies for his specimen collection. He looked at Malcolm in horror, picturing his brother pinned onto a cork square in a display cabinet.

"Run Oswald screamed at the top of his voice. "Wake up Malcolm! Run for your bloody life!" But Malcolm remained rooted to the spot, a serene expression on his face and a far away look in his eyes. He could have been listening peacefully to the Hallelujah Chorus at the church concert.

The wizard turned defiantly to face the robot. "You've hypnotised them all. Try hypnotising me you murderous tin can! You can't let me get away. I must be the most interesting specimen you've ever met." He threw out that desperate challenge, hoping to gain time.

The clown just laughed at him.

Oswald was desperate. He tried to use his magic. He directed all his power at the clown, hoping to destroy him or upset his artificial brain with another of his heating spells. The turf caught fire at the robot's feet, curling and crackling with the intensity of the magic. Delicate spirals of glowing grass rose into the air around the metal man, but he was completely unharmed by it. In desperation Oswald turned his attention to his surroundings. He stared at the bandstand. It caught fire instantly. Bright yellow flames leapt into the dark night from the thatched roof. The timber floor and the side rails, well soaked with years of creosote, crackled and spat as they burned. He hoped the fire brigade would see the flames and investigate. Maybe someone else in the town would notice the fire and come to look. Black smoke curled up towards the alien spacecraft that hovered above them. The acrid smoke was so thick, it temporarily blotted out the beam of light focused on the park.

"Enough of this foolery," the clown commanded impatiently. "It is time I taught you a lesson." The robot stared hard at Oswald and an intense green light began to dance behind its hypnotic eyes.

Oswald bravely stood his ground. He cleared his mind and gathered his thoughts to defend himself, but he could feel the robot's gaze searching for an opening in his defences, probing his brain like an expert swordsman with a rapier. Slowly he felt the power of the clown's thought waves increase to an intensity almost impossible to resist.

The Wizard knew he would eventually lose the contest. He knew the robot was much too powerful. No mere human could hope to stand in its way when the blighter was so determined to win. In desperation the Wizard tried one last ploy. He relaxed and gave in, inviting the robot's mind to enter his own.

The clown felt his adversary crumbling. He pushed home his advantage and entered the Wizard's mind unhampered. There he started to search through Oswald's memory cells, curious to see what peculiar kind of human intellect had given him so much trouble.

Oswald concentrated all his thoughts on one single image. He pictured the schoolroom at Runford Grammar School where he had studied as a boy. There was the blackboard on the wall and his old maths master, writing on it. In thick white chalk letters he imagined his old teacher writing a mathematical formula on the blackboard.

'The answer to the riddle of the universe is the value of Pi. That value we calculate from the formula for the area of a circle.' This intriguing statement was followed by the algebraic formula.

The intruder in the Wizard's mind hesitated in front of the blackboard, read the chalked message, then turned to the door of the next imaginary classroom and moved into that chamber. Oswald kept his nerve and rebuilt the image exactly as it had been before. There was the blackboard and beside it stood his old maths master, tattered black gown on his thin shoulders and chalk stick in his bony hand. Each time the robot turned to another part of the Wizard's mind he found himself facing the same wise looking gowned figure standing beside the same blackboard with the very same message chalked on it.

Oswald held his breath and clenched his fists. He had gambled on the robot not knowing the mathematical value of Pi and not understanding the implications of it. He was counting on the fact that the clown was only an information gathering robot and not mathematically inclined. The Wizard felt the intruder hesitate, then he felt him concentrate on the bogus statement, written large on the wall of every imaginary room.

As soon as the robot swallowed the bait and began to calculate the answer to the mathematical formula, the pressure eased. It was like a great weight being lifted off his shoulders. The Wizard knew, as every schoolboy knows, the answer to that particular mathematical question is infinitely long. It is impossible to complete the calculation. The digits go on forever. That's why an approximation is always used. The most complex computer known would go on to the end of time, producing an endless string of numbers as the answer to the equation. The computation would take from now to eternity.

Peter Piper calculated in a frenzy, putting more and more of his free memory banks to the task. Oswald felt the foreign presence withdraw completely from his mind. The robot believed it was locked on to the answer to the riddle of the universe and everything else was irrelevant to it. The machine stood motionless, a look of intense concentration on its synthetic features as it tried to capture this priceless information for its masters.

At last the sleepwalkers reacted to this slip in the clown's control. They began to move listlessly and to wake up. They yawned. They stretched. Finally, they all opened their eyes and stare around the park and at each other.

"Good God! Freda, where am I?" Malcolm shouted into the night air. "Who left that fridge door open? It's cold in here." He shivered and pulled his pyjama jacket tightly about himself.

"Hello! Hello! Hello! That bathing suit is a wee bit skimpy." Poole exclaimed as he came face to face with Mavis Peabody's bare body.

"Well! I'll go to the foot of the Giants Causeway! If it isn't a wee man riding up and down." Michael Flannegan had spotted Fred Hinman sitting on his bicycle, dressed only in his nightshirt.

"Ooh! I've never seen anything like that before!" Mavis Peabody screeched as she spotted the robot's metal aerial dangling down past his knees.

At that precise moment the brownies woke up. In her confusion Vickie rushed over to the clown to ask him to do another Punch and Judy show.

Blackie, who was enjoying savaging the rats in the flowerbeds, stopped and glanced up at the sound of Vickie's familiar voice. The cat took one look at the robot and instinctively knew that something was wrong.

The space ship emitted a high pitched whine as it manoeuvred above the park. It was a timely reminder of their imminent danger. Oswald looked up apprehensively and saw it was drawing much closer to them. Strange shadowy shapes were silhouetted against the light and could be seen looking down from the open hatch.

"Run for your lives, everybody!" Oswald yelled at the waking sleepwalkers. "Don't just stand there. Bloody well run or you'll be crunched by that falling aeroplane!"

All of them except Vickie, looked up at the bright light descending on their heads, and scattered across the park. She seemed spellbound by the light and the presence of the clown.

Blackie did not hesitate. She bounded across the park and knocked the robot off its feet. Grabbing Vickie by the collar, as if lifting a kitten by the scruff of its neck, she dashed of with her to safety.

Oswald dived for the nearest flowerbed and hid among the bushes. When he eventually peeped out he was relieved to see the robot lying alone in the centre of a circle of intense white light. Peter Piper looked exactly like the lone compere of a Royal Command performance. The shaft of light from the flying bowler hat, narrowed onto its target.

"Beam me up, Scottie." Peter cackled in a drunken Irish voice. The metal robot rose into the air and accelerated up to its mother ship like a silver plastic bag, sucked up an invisible vacuum cleaner tube. The space ship's propulsion units revved loudly. Suddenly it was gone.

Oswald walked over to the scorched grass ring where the Pied Piper had stood and examined the area curiously. He bent down and picked up the objects he found there. The Punch and Judy puppets he kept in his hand for Fred Hinman, but the suit and the three cornered black and white hat, made of a peculiar metallic plastic material, he folded small and stuffed into his pocket for future investigation.

The Wizard looked up at the Milky Way. The stars and moon were back where they belonged. All traces of the alien space ship and the information gathering robot were gone.

Runford Park was silent, except for the rustle and chatter of the bemused sleepwalkers.

"I suppose it's up to me to round that lot up, hypnotise them again and send them back to their homes." He looked at the bemused collection of locals.

"Right you lot. Gather round me. I've something important to tell you." Oswald took out his pocket watch and swung it on the gold chain in front of their eyes.

"Back to sleep...to sleep...to sleep..." Probably because they had not yet woken up properly, more than the efficacy of the wizard's hypnosis technique, they all quickly succumbed to his suggestions and their eyes closed.

"Back home. Everyone of you."   Oswald

ordered. "Back to your beds and remember nothing of this in the morning."

Slowly the adults walked from the park, like zombies leaving a late night party. Each one made for home as the Wizard had ordered. The children were another matter. They climbed into the Range Rover and sat waiting for Vickie to drive them back.

"Oh God! Vickie Giles has vanished!" Oswald slapped the palm of his open hand on his forehead in despair. Just when he thought he had it all under control, this had to happen. He remembered seeing the Black Panther leap on the robot and save the girl but where had they gone after that?

"Here Kitty-kitty." He called in desperation, but there was no sign of either of them.

Chapter Twenty Seven

Oswald would have preferred to escort Tina back home, Lydia back to the Dog in a Doublet or even Mavis Peabody to the flat above the chip shop, but his conscience wouldn't let him. There were several lost Brownies sitting in Will Giles Range Rover by the park gate, and no one to get them home. He resigned himself to doing one last good turn and took on the job of chauffeur.

The girls were very helpful. They told Oswald which way to go and where to stop to drop them off. Within half an hour he had reduced the load to one girl, who lived only half a mile from the Giles farmhouse. He waved goodbye to the last passenger and was just turning the car around to drive back to Runford when he spotted a pair of glowing green eyes coming along the road towards him. He sank down behind the wheel, switched off the engine and waited.

Along the road came Blackie. The big cat was trotting steadily along the grass verge with something on her back. Oswald strained his eyes to see what was coming. Suddenly, in the car headlights he realised it was Vickie Giles sitting astride the big cat and hanging onto its neck. When the cat drew level with the Range Rover, the girl slid off its back and walked to the car.

"Psst! Get in, Vickie. I'll drive you home." Oswald whispered to the girl.

The cat's ears stood erect at the sound of this voice. Vickie, who had not been among the crowd when they were hypnotised again, realised at once that it was Oswald.

"Hello, Mr Gotobed. I'm glad I've found you. I was worried how I was going to explain to dad about his car."

"Get in, Vickie." Oswald pushed the passenger door open.

"What about Blackie?"

Oswald scratched his head. What about Blackie? The cat wouldn't trust him enough to get into the car with them. In fact the animal was already wandering off and beginning to melt into the darkness surrounding them. He had a sudden inspiration.

"Wind down your window and call her to follow us. I'll drive slowly so she can keep up with us."

Oswald and Vickie led the big cat back to her father's farm.

"Now Vickie. If we can persuade Blackie to go into the barn, I may be able to get her back to her correct size. And I know where she's left her kittens."

Vickie stood in the beam of the car headlights and called the cat to her. Oswald stayed well out of sight. They had just managed to persuade the cat to go into the barn when a light went on in an upstairs window of the farmhouse.

"Quick. Lock the cat in and give me the key. Leave the talking to me, Vickie."

Oswald put on his thinking cap and thought up a plan, double quick.

"Whose that in the yard?" A gun barrel poked out of the upstairs window as Will Giles gruff voice bellowed the question at them.

"Tell him its you." Oswald hissed at the girl.

"Its only me, dad."

"Not again! ..."

The sound of bolts could be heard as the back door was unlocked. Oswald stood and held the child's hand, crossing the fingers of his other hand, behind his back, hoping his story would be believed.

"Back up everything I tell him. And please don't mention Blackie!" He hissed out of the corner of his mouth.

Will Giles stepped into the yard, his gun resting over his arm. He was amazed to find his daughter and the druggist standing by the Range Rover.

"Hello! What's going on here, Mr Gotobed?"

"Oh! …er hello Will…I found your daughter fast asleep in town. She was in your car. I reckon she must have driven herself to Runford in her sleep. Yes…that's it…she must have driven in her sleep."

Will scratched his head in disbelief and tried to understand what was being said.

"I drove her back here, in case you were worried about her."

"But she's too young to drive." Will was still wrestling with the enormity of the situation.

"No she's not!" Mrs Giles stepped out of the door behind him. "You're to blamed for this. You would teach her to drive the car across the fields. She asked me of she could drive in town the other day." She held out her arms to her daughter.

Vickie rushed to her mother and hugged her. They both burst into tears.

"Ahem! Ahem!" Oswald cleared his throat to remind them he was still there and miles from home. "Do you think someone could run me home? I drove your car and the girl here, bit I've no way of getting back."

"Come into the kitchen and have a coffee while I get dressed." Will ushered them all indoors.

Mrs Giles made a coffee for the three adults and

a hot chocolate for Vickie.

"We shall have to lock her bedroom window until she grows out of this sleepwalking," she told her husband. "And we shall have to leave any driving lessons until she's old enough."

Will looked sheepishly at his wife and nodded.

"Goodnight and thank you, Mr Gotobed." Vickie reached over and kissed him on the cheek.

Oswald hugged her close to him and whispered in her ear. "No mention of Blackie. Don't forget."

Will turned the car around and drove Oswald home to his front door.

Once the Range Rover was out of sight, Oswald rushed into his kitchen and grabbed the remains of the reducing spell he had made for the big cat. He scooped up the kittens and sealed them in a cardboard box, then he donned his motorbike gear and hurried out of the house Oswald strapped the box containing the kittens onto his pillion seat and drove his motorbike to the Giles farm. By that time of the morning, It was already beginning to get light in the east, as the dawn approached. He knew he had to work fast if he was to return Blackie to her normal size in time.

At the farm, Oswald parked in the lane and sprinted to the yard, carrying the cat's young family in his arms. He stopped at the back of the barn and untied the box. The kittens were wide awake and crying to be fed.

Inside the barn, the big cat heard the kitten's cries and answered with a roar of its own. Oswald felt the wooden barn shudder as Blackie threw herself against the inside wall, attempting to get to her litter.

"God! Stop that, Blackie. You'll wake the whole damn neighbourhood!" he grunted.

The cat clawed at the wall again.

Oswald was desperate. He knew he had one slim chance to put things right. If he failed, Will Giles would force the barn door open and find the panther inside! That was unthinkable. Some one or something would get hurt.

In desperation, Oswald took the reducing potion from his pocket and poured it on the kittens fur. If only the cat would lick her brood she would get the potion and she might just grow small again. He rubbed the liquid into the kittens' fur, and felt in his pocket for the barn key.

Oswald knew that opening the barn door to push the litter inside, would be the trickiest part of the whole plan. He tiptoed to the door, turned the key in the lock and pulled the wooden door slightly open. At first he could hear nothing of the cat inside, but suddenly there was a loud thump as Blackie jumped at the door and pushed against it!

Oswald had to put his boot and all his weight against the open door to hold it just ajar. He grabbed the kittens and thrust them through the small slit. Blackie backed off when her litter appeared. Before the cat could get over its surprise, the Wizard slammed the door shut and turned the key in the lock.

"Phew! Thank God for that!" Oswald was just congratulating himself on a difficult mission accomplished, when a man's voice bellowed at him from the farm .

"Whose out there? What d'ya want?"

It was Will Giles and he sounded angry! Oswald ran for cover just in time. Will opened the window and discharged both barrels of his shotgun at the barn door.

"Grief! That was close." Oswald scrambled to his feet and sprinted to his motor bike. In seconds he was speeding back along the fen road, heading for home, his bed and a few hours sleep.

Next morning brought raging doubts for the Wizard. He lay awake looking at the ceiling and wondering if the cat had licked the kittens clean, or if she had once again ignored them. He prayed that being locked in the barn with them, she had overcome her doubts and washed them with her tongue. She certainly seemed to know their cries when she heard them.

By breakfast time he knew what had to be done. He must take the day off from work and go out to see the Giles family. He telephoned his brother and made an excuse for being off for the day, then rode his motorbike back to the farm.

"Hello, Mr Gotobed. That was a busy night you had last night." Mrs Giles greeted him as he drove into the yard.

"Yes. How is your daughter this morning?"

"Tired, but otherwise OK. We've let her stay off school today to catch up on her sleep."

As they were talking Oswald glanced over at the barn door to see if anyone had opened it. He saw the key was still in the lock and the doors were closed. That relieved his anxieties in one way, but added to his worries in another.

"Eh up, Mr Gotobed. Can't you keep away from the place?" Will Giles came into the yard.

"Oh yes. Just called to see if your daughter was alright. That was a funny business last night."

"You're telling me! We shall have to put a bell round her neck to tell us where she is."

An upstairs window opened and Vickie waved down at them. Morning, Mr Gotobed. How's Blackie this morning?"

Oswald frowned at her, trying to remind her to keep quiet about the cat. She put her hand over her mouth.

"She'll be down in a minute. You'll be able to see for yourself that she's no worse for her night out." Will chuckled. "Do you want a cup of tea? I'm just going to have one." They all walked into the kitchen.

Vickie joined them in the kitchen and ate her breakfast then she and Oswald walked out into the yard.

"I dreamed that Blackie was huge and she gave me ride on her back." The girl eyed her companion quizzically. "It was a dream, wasn't it, Mr Gotobed?"

"Must have been." Oswald lied, but he avoided her gaze as he said it.

"I can't help thinking that Blackie is really a Black Panther and she's locked in the barn." The child looked at him again with her large innocent eyes.

"That would make a good story to tell your friends. You have some imagination there. You'll be able to write about it at school." Oswald swallowed hard and crossed his fingers behind his back.

Vickie broke off their conversation and ran to the barn.

"I'm going to see for myself, she shouted over her shoulder.

Oswald started towards her but he was far too slow. She had the lock undone and the door flung open before he could move. He stood rooted to the spot and prayed fervently as the girl vanished inside the barn.

Time passed inexorably slowly. Oswald's life passed before his eyes. Everything he had ever regretted rushed into his mind. He broke out in a cold sweat.

"Oh! Do come and look, Mr Gotobed." Vickie called excitedly from inside the building.

Oswald walked reluctantly to the barn, not daring to believe his plan had worked.

Aren't they lovely! Three kittens. Two like their mum and one pure white." The girl held the small furry bundles in her arms.

Oswald turned to look for the kittens' mother. There was a cry from near his feet. He felt Blackie brushing herself against his leg. He couldn't believe his eyes! She was back to her normal size and she remembered him. He almost cried with relief.

"I suppose all that fun with a clown and a space ship and a Black Panther was all my imagination. I did enjoy the dream though."

Oswald put his arm around the girl's shoulder and hugged her to him. If only she knew the truth!